'The stories in *Saints* are
and attentive in their depic
destructive impulses of the human heart.'

Colin Barrett

'This handful of offbeat lives, their vivid Mexican setting, their human light and shade, are so well rendered they offer a sense of special access to other realities. As in life, each story is a wormhole to the next, a connectivity that not only makes a novel of this collection but inflates its reading to four dimensions, with all the discovery that comes from entering a new milieu in person. For me this book does the heavy lifting of literature: more than a good read – it's a parallel life.'

D.B.C. Pierre

Tim MacGabhann works from an imaginative world that does not rest. His living characters open up their hearts to him, and he reports back to us - a work of sublime devotion to a place and a moment that has been rendered in perfect detail. I go back to these stories long after reading them, and wonder how those people are. It's a sweet and violent magic, and I remain gladly under its spell.

Ben Pester

SAINTS

Tim MacGabhann

First published in 2025
by Scratch Books Ltd.
London

The moral rights of the author of this book
to be identified as such is asserted in accordance with the
Copyright, Designs and Patents Act of 1988.

Tim MacGabhann © 2025 by Scratch Books

Jacket design: Alice Haworth-Booth
Image adapted from 'Statue of Xochipilli' by Antony Stanley,
licensed under CC BY-SA 2.0. flickr.com/photos/antonystanley
Typesetting: Will Dady

All rights reserved. No part of this publication may
be reproduced, stored in a retrieval system, or transmitted in any
form or by any means, electronic, mechanical photocopying, recording,
or otherwise, without the prior permission of both the copyright
owner and the above publisher of this book.

Printed and bound on carbon-balanced paper in the UK by CMP Books

ISBN 978-1-0683555-1-6

Contents

Chair	9
Satellite	23
Better	41
Cleaner	57
Beach	79
Dive	97
Chefs	117
Saints	139
Bodies	161

SAINTS

CHAIR

1.

I live on a roof, in an old maids' quarters: a shed-sized concrete homelet right there between the cisterns and the bird cages. Two floors down is the room where I chair Narcotics Anonymous meetings three days a week. But I'm not in there now. I am hauling bags of sand one at a time from beneath the stairs. I am just always trying to make less stuff happen all the time. What this stops happening is it stops the place flooding. Dragging the bags is a pain in the ass. The door is too heavy to hold open with my foot. So I drag the bag as far as the door, drop the bag, open the door, go out the door, push the door open from the far side, hold the door against my shoulder, haul the bag with one hand, dump the bag. Then I go back through the door as far as the stairs, go under the stairs, check the bottom seam of the next bag, take the roll of tape from the corner of the space under the stairs where I had the tape, lay a strip along the seam if the seam looks weak, pull at the tape with my teeth, then drag the bag as far as the door, drop the bag, open the door, go out the door, push the door open from the far side, and so on; the ache in my shoulders and lower back becoming a burn in my shoulders and lower back and finally a numbness in my shoulders and lower back, until the bags are all laid out in a big 'C' that begins at the left-hand lintel of the sex shop to the right of the door to the meeting room, and the little stand of chips and cigarettes and mints and chewing gum owned by the old woman, to the left hand lintel of the hipster pulquería, stopping before their door because I hate their door, because the doormen there wear these weird all-black contact lenses like the guitarist in Limp Bizkit used to have and always tell me the prices of their drinks and to come on in, on rote, like bots, like one day I might go in there.

The problem of dragging the bags doesn't end just with which lintel to draw the 'C' from. The problem of the 'C' itself poses problems, in that as the 'C' grows I must jink in and around the pedestrians – office types with lanyards swinging, eyes on their phones, workers toting gallons of water on their shoulders, bike couriers going ninety, tourists at bovine speed, with bovine loudness, in bovine numbers – and take their looks and their tongue-clicks and their head-shakes with the kind of mute placidity that is meant to obliterate resentment but sometimes only presses the resentment flatter within me.

The 'C' goes three bags high. The pedestrians butt their shins or their knees on the 'C' or else hurdle the 'C' entirely. It's not like it's my fucking fault. It's the fault of the government; they're the ones who took a stone head of the rain god Tlaloc from his crag above a valley in Otomí territory. These stone heads marked the heights people watched the clouds gather at, if the clouds were of a specific darkness there then they would know if they were to plant, or sow, or dig flood channels, or flee for higher ground. Unpegging those stone heads from the mountain unpegged the people from the seasons and the seasons from time itself. Now the world just grows old by itself, everything flies apart, the rains get worse year on year, fall punctually at the worst of rush hour, so that if I don't lay my 'C' of sandbags the old woman's stall will wash away and the sex shop will flood and my building with the meeting in it will flood and nobody will be able to get in and up the stairs for the meeting.

Flip through the fat-white vellum of the old annals at the city's main library, those big books that thud open, flake-edged scab-crimson leather, and you'll find any number of floods: 1607, when an eight-mile incision in the earth was needed to drain the floodwaters; the thirty-six straight hours of rain that fell in 1629, pummelling the corn-stalks to nothing, crumbling the adobe houses, reducing the main square to a tiny island stalked by rabid dogs who snapped their jaws at any boat that got close enough; and 1692, which brought a mud-slide so bad that people resorted to canoes instead of pack animals. Everything wheeled was abandoned, just as in the days before the Spanish. Masses were held, priests imploring the skies from the roofs of churches in front of congregations gathered in little boats. There have been so many ends of the world here. Europe's the incision through which the whole continent is bleeding to death. I test the sandbag with the toe of my boot.

The thing about apocalyptic visions is they always exempt the visionary. I'm not exempt from shit. I'm going down too. These bags won't hold forever. One day the rains'll close over my roof. I'll sink and be gone in a pluming of dirt-coloured bubbles. They'll catch up with me eventually, maybe, the years using. Lungs clear, liver unbruised, kidneys as glossy as a pair of beans, all that, but who's to say when the post will return from all of those other times of huffing stuff off foil, or banging up, or drinking for years, even from the toxins in the tinfoil, blowing in little subatomic ribbons around my brain, mercury-shimmers waiting to fatally catch somewhere in there.

The only person not doing that stressed-commuter jog through the wet is one of the crack sadhus who lives in the little triangular park between two big cross-streets. He goes picking through the crowd, a holy slowness to his gait, a wry smile on his face. He watches the adverts repeat themselves silently, endlessly, in morphing shapes of heated plasma, locked inside the walled garden of his little chemical heaven.

When the 'C' is laid out, I stand with my hands on my hips and my foot on top of a bag and watch the crack guy for a while, and then I squint up at the rainclouds, trying to read something in its darkness that isn't just 'A fuck ton of rain is about to fall', and feel a dark ache leak from my back.

2.

Paper lanterns sway in the blue gloom, outside the Chinese restaurant where I'm waiting for the rain to stop. The metal roof of this restaurant is really roaring. It's got everything else on mute: the sputter of oil coming from the kitchen, the bubbling of the fish-tank filter behind me where koi nudge through the murk, the rasp of the fraying electric wires coiled at the top of a pole on the corner. I'm looking across at the sandbag barricade, my foot tapping, hoping they'll hold. The bottom sandbag's dark with rain, phosphor around the edges, all these little white bubbles. But the old woman in the snacks stand looks cosy and serene under her umbrella, her steel-grey braids immaculate. If she's feeling OK then I should feel OK.

My notebook has my step work in it. Step work is when you get the big Narcotics Anonymous manual with the green and gold cover and go question-by-question through all twelve of the steps, beginning to end, like the book's interviewing you: *What does 'the disease of addiction' mean to you? Has your disease been active recently? In what way? What is it like when you're obsessed with something? Does your thinking follow a pattern?*

I've been going back to this book for seven years. Looking at my answers, I just see words now. I am always just trying to stop more stuff happen. What writing all this down does is stop my head chewing on itself, throw some language into those teeth, giving them something to gnaw on, gnash through, chomp to mush, before they come after me again.

I lean back against the lilac-and-turquoise pleather banquette. My knuckles rap the table. I can hear my mouth and throat making a stressed little *hm hm hm* noise, even if my body doesn't quite feel stressed, not all the way. Eels of lit rain unthread from umbrella rims. Milky tints roil kerbside and vapour chases cars through the drench. Little frost-beads of hung rain deck the market-stalls. Steam unfurls in crisp layers from hot-plates, ruby lights vie and shimmy all down Insurgentes.

If I go out now my jeans'll be an otter's pelt in seconds. I've no umbrella, and there's an hour to go to the meeting. But I need to get donuts. The pedestrians out there legging it through the foam, the Hindu-god tangle of the arms I can see through the bus windows, the people leaning on the horns, the people coming to the meeting, about to flop forward through the door in their wet-dog smell of soaked jumpers and jeans and find warmth, peace, coffee, sugar, and the thought of them coming in and not finding any of those things makes my gut squirm: on day one, if I'd come in, found none of that, maybe I'd have bounced out, picked up, gone way off the deep end, lain around for days and days getting rotty, feeling like if I got out of bed the paint on the boards was going to blister and curl and pop in little bubbles so dark were the hate waves beaming off me, milling stimulus into myself, trying to get to that numb and reckless place in myself. Only thing that'd work sometimes was I'd get up and do just one thing very very carefully: something like opening a pomegranate over a bowl. That'd take up all my attention. Peeling off the skin so none burst. Working the little red jewels out of the pith without them mashing under my thumbs. Little ping of the unbroken ones falling into the ceramic. And then the taste. Oh, wow. I could spend half an hour peeling one. More, even, anytime my ex was annoyed at me. I'd put them in a little bowl. Really careful, no pith, none of the little dud brown ones, either – just a glittering garnet heap. And then a sliced lemon on the side.

I stir in another sugar and I squint out at the rain. It's a white fog. It's whatever.

I can afford to get soaked once in a while. It beats getting my hands all sticky opening a fucking pomegranate with my scalp prickling with sweat and my hands shaking like a Bargaintown wardrobe.

I get up. Leave a note under the saucer. Out into the wet, eyes shut, the spray on my face, just this one big sea coming at me, skirling with brakes and roaring with wind and truck wheels. And it's completely fine.

3.

In the donut shop, the woman at the till boxes up the one dozen cajeta rings, turns the card terminal towards me and says, 'You really get through these.'

Hail pings down. The rattle is like a snare-drum. The ankles of my jeans drip. So does my fringe. Drops patter on the counter.

'I watch a lot of football,' I say, and type in my PIN.

4.

All the way up the street from the donut shop I wear the plastic bag on my head and hold my jacket in a wing over the donut box and dodge and jink through everyone and past a scooter taking one of those right turns I hate. I even stand back for a couple of people once or twice, slam myself flat against the insides of doorways, against walls like I'm in a videogame, with so many puddles to hop, so many missing chunks of pavement, so many trails of downed phone wire, so many bits of protruding pipe that don't make any fucking sense whatsoever. But then I'm under the shelter again in the sickly pink glow of the sex shop, and the sandbag barricade is not foaming around the bottom in a telltale leak of dirty brown sand, and the relief I feel in my chest is like the bottom of a boxing ring snapping, that big taut beige cloth giving away, dropping me into something like freedom. I hop the sandbags. I pat the top one like it's the flank of a horse and it's warm. I go back inside. I go upstairs. I lay the cracked laminates with the opening readings out on the chairs, one apiece: *Just for Today*, *How It Works*, *The Twelve Traditions*, *Who Is an Addict*, *What is the NA Program*, *We Do Recover*, intro spiels on sallowing paper from the drag of so many hands, the plastic darkened, cracked, flaking.

Here's how a meeting goes: we come in, read the intros for ten minutes or so, read a bit of the *Big Book*, or *Living Clean* or whatever I've been able to order in over the Internet, and then for the last forty minutes we share about the stuff we've read, or on whatever's making us feel like shit and want to relapse, or even on just any good quiet things that happened. I hold the laminate with the last of the intro texts, titled *We Do Recover*, and look at it for a second. I barely know what the word 'recovery' means anymore: it fibres into synonyms if I think too hard – 'make up ground', 'make up for', 'compensate', 'get better', 'get back'. What we get back I don't know. You get to talk for three minutes and listen for fifty-seven when you're in a meeting. I am just always trying to make less stuff happen all the time. What the listening stops happening is it stops me from feeling like I'm in a story where stuff's happening and instead like I'm standing on a narrow bank between two rivers where stories surge past, big muscular currents teeming with bubbles, but none of it pulling me away.

5.

I tip coffee into the percolator. I make a mandala of Oreos with donuts around the rim. I am just always trying to make less stuff happen all the time. What this does is it stops people turning up at the meeting all chippy and dyspeptic from Metro cram and traffic peristalsis and the buzz of the pavements, it stops them having a shit day and then a shit meeting and then a shit night, and then turn that out on the person nearest them.

Next, I take the school-chairs one by one off the pile and put them in a ring, too, until the whole room – biscuits, donut, plate, chairs – lines up with the pattern of the tapestry on the wall, gold wheels within gold wheels on rippling deep red, fading towards a hazy white centre.

Frayed strings show through the surface of the carpet. It needs replacing. So does everything. The walls shake with the club next door – Depeche Mode, The Cure – kids dressed up in stuff that's old but feels new to them.

My alarm beeps: two minutes till the meeting. I get out the little pyx-sized wicker basket for the donations that go on rent and literature. I get out the little bell I ring when someone's got less than a minute of their time left to share. I flip open the ledger, open the blue *Big Book* to the marker, shape out the daily reading with my lips so's I can read it steadily when the meeting's on. I take the chair behind the little chipped blue desk, shut my eyes, sit, listen. The percolator's snoring, the laminates are all laid out, and my cup's brimming with coffee so strong the bubbles have a little oil-stain shine to them.

6.

On the sill, our plants, their smell: warm, wetted gravel, saturated muck. On the roof I've got cucharilla and agave and San Pedro and órgano cactus, glass and tile mosaics on their pots, which bring hummingbirds and big yellow-black butterflies. White rainy-season skies like a blank page, the parks' banana and palm trees soaked in the rain-fog, air gauzy with pollen, pollution, downpour. For millions of years the valley was a huge, reefed, inland lake.

The only story was the deep hiss of water receding from stone, pitted rock weeping drops, billowing fog: just like now, the bus lane undulant with a slush of hail and water, the buses crashing as they speed past, leaf-cool, deep with time, history reduced to sensation, to a fog cool on the forearms, as though all that lost water were suspended in the air, the ghost of the lake the Spanish drained, waiting to come back. It's hard not to think that maybe it is coming back, in a way we don't want maybe, but coming back all the same. Sometimes nothing is lost: not even lake.

The stories in these meetings end one of three ways – jails, institutions, death – though just sometimes there's a twist, a miracle, and nobody dies at the end. Any way on and any way through can be a way back if you frame it right. I reach and open the window and let the raincool in, spritzing my wet wrists with fresher wetness.

7.

Downstairs the door squeaks open. A clatter, a rustle: someone shaking raindrops from an umbrella. Feet clop up steps. I get up. I go to the door, so that whoever's there can come through, get a donut, sit down, and say, *I'm Anabelle and I'm an addict, I'm Miguel and I'm an addict, I'm Alejandro and I'm an addict, I'm Adonai and I'm an addict, I'm Lucio and I'm an addict, I'm Helena and I'm an addict—*

SATELLITE

Alejandro kicks his bike into life and roars off into the pre-dawn gloom, sting of fresh air rippling up the sleeves of his jacket. The blast of the exhaust leaves yesterday in a tatter behind him – bad head pictures, a homeless kid, arms and neck and face mottled with dirt, one eye gone, the rim around the gone eye a reddish mash. The cashier'd used a .45 on him: who did he think he was, Charles Bronson? Defending an Oxxo with a .45. Where he'd even gotten it Alejandro didn't want to know – he didn't believe the cashier had found it in a bin. Things were bad but not so bad that .45s were turning up in bins in Roma Sur.

But that's Monday's problem: now the city is receding below him, the road empty, his head empty too, like he's in an ad: insurance, maybe, or phones, those flat images of freedom – now his, only his. He loves the snug way his helmet holds his head together and he loves the view around him. He never gets to see the city like this – a split opal, he thinks, all those lights. He usually sees it as a gut shape on a map rashed all over with the little stickers: grey for assault, red for rape, black for murder. Yesterday's one on the corner of Motolinía and Independencia. He stood there arms folded, breathing slow, looking at the black disc until the striplights hummed and the yellow lino seemed to pulse and the walls sucked in and out in time with his lungs.

But then the moment passed and he wrote the date on the black sticker in white pen.

He's timed it perfectly. A Chinese satellite is due to drop out of space and land in the sea off Coatzacoalcos, and he is going to get there on his bike just in time to watch it. He took a slice of cake Teresa from forensics left him. She and her wife have him over more since his wife moved out. Maybe it's nice for them, too: the weight of their silences has something like the leaden lull he remembers.

The quick poetry of making ready – throw off the tarp, wax the bike, fill the tank, fill the jerrican, fold the tarp, swim, eat, wash, leave, in such a burn to be down there on the sand, to watch the sea boil and whiten, watch everything coming apart, like the dead kid from yesterday, separated into practice-parts for UNAM medical students, the report on his death gathering the first layers of its permanent nap of dust. Everything in its right place. The parts rest nowhere important, but aren't entirely lost either, except into processes which, while not perfect, are at least civic or functional in their intention.

The idea about going to see the satellite came to him one night he was half-watching Discovery – meteor strikes, miles of grass and forest gouged with long silver drags, melted slag and ore. He'd felt a big rolling shiver carry up his body, his blood steaming, the feeling of Chixculub's massive white flash, the wet ripping noise of vines and tree-trunks cindering, noise enough to drown the bellow of every incinerated dinosaur.

'The earth is hit by a hundred and forty thousand tonnes of rock from space every single year,' said the astronomer, 'it's best to picture the Earth as an apple on a string, turning and turning, a thousand assault rifles shooting at it from afar.'

The screen showed the stone turning end over end through space, bean-shaped like the birthmark on his heel – a good-luck press of the thumb, his mother used to say, from an older brother who didn't make it to term.

He doesn't drink or do drugs anymore so the drifty, fever motion of his thoughts when the bike's under him is the closest he can get to being out of it. Yesterday's smog is still thick and the lights on the towers are all still on. From up here, he can see layer after layer of the mountains. He sees the point of the satellite as bright as a needle, its debris scoring a pink line across the sky, though he forces himself back to the drone of tyres on tarmac.

He doesn't stop until it's time for a piss in a clearing off a forested stretch of road. Zen is pissing to piss. Zen is doing plus nothing, washing the dishes plus nothing, riding the motorbike plus nothing, washing the dishes just to wash the dishes, riding the motorbike just to ride the motorbike.

Zen emptiness is his thing these days. The apartment he lives in was the showroom for the whole building – fully furnished with the blandest imaginable shit from Ikea. No other cop he knows could afford all of this, but no other cop he knows was pensioned off by the Marines. He loves the wipe-clean shine of his beige sofas, the kitchen island identical to the one in the billboard outside, the framed photos of canyons and sunsets. Only one photo taken down and stowed behind the couch – desert road, blinding sky, the sand pocked with ocotillo and saguaro, the fence-posts parched and split – too much like the place where his division found the missing cadets. From the helicopter, their arms and legs almost spelled out letters. Up close, they no longer smelled: vultures and coyotes had left only scraps, lips scorched to thin black seams like melted rubber. Bagging them up, Alejandro watched the vultures overhead, a big, slow rhyme with the turning rotors.

This is the only memory he hasn't been able to keep away. So that isn't so bad.

The back wall of the clearing is a cracked sheet of limestone stretching way up into the trees. He has one foot on a shaky rock and the other on the ground, and some tightness to the muscle puts a spot of warmth under the birthmark on his heel. He doesn't know what his brother would think of what he's done with this life that was meant to do for two of them, and he's about to stoop, lift the cuff of his jeans, and press his own thumb to the spot, when a heron arrows silently past his nose, out from one stand of firs, into another.

Alejandro sits in the roadside café halfway to Coatzacoalcos in front of a plate of chilaquiles, mixing his fork in long slow circles – the sauce, the cream, the crumbly white cheese melting in gluey zeroes within the greenish morass. He's left acres of lingering time between now and the satellite hitting the atmosphere.

A voice says, 'Sorry to bother you, but, eh', and looks up and sees a thin, youngish man – one-point-eight metres, fifty-five kilos, hair brown, green eyes, pale brown skin, nervous, palms up, unarmed – who coagulates before him though not fully; he has white marks like cracks in his face, as though the plates of his skull aren't holding together. Alejandro feels his stomach growl in protest.

'What is it, chief?' says Alejandro.

'Don't mind me asking where you're going, do you?' says the youngish man. He's already pulling out the chair and sitting down.

Alejandro brings his hands together. Zen is doing plus nothing. Which is a shit idea if you have to think of two things at once, such as having breakfast and also getting to Coatzacoalcos in time for a Chinese satellite planking into the sea.

'Why?' Alejandro says.

'Well,' says the youngish man, hands locked together, too. Alejandro looks at his wrists, swallows, looks away. The youngish man turns towards the door and says, 'It's my bus. We stopped for a break. But I got out of the bathroom and it's left without me.'

Alejandro looks past his shoulder, through the door at the bluish pines swaying in the wind. The weather app said it'd be bright. He lifts his fork and takes a bite while it's hot.

'I just saw you'd the bike,' says the youngish man, gesturing with his thumb. 'Thought maybe. Well. We catch it up.'

'You've the ticket?' Alejandro says, as he chews.

The youngish man pats his pockets.

'Fuck,' he says. 'No. But it's a big bus. Grey.'

Alejandro shuts his eyes, says, 'Going where?' The gentleness in his voice is the same he puts on at work, a gentleness that tickles the suspect's ribs like the tip of a knife; the same gentleness when he's trying not to hammer the suspect's head to a reddish mash against the concrete floor.

'Coatzacoalcos,' says the youngish man. 'There's this—'

'Satellite,' says Alejandro, scooping up more food. 'Yes, I know.'

'I was going to ask,' the youngish man says. 'I wanted. If you could. Catch the bus.'

'We won't do that,' says Alejandro, hunkering forwards over his plate. The old woman running the place approaches the table, drying her hands on a black tea towel with *CANCÚN* stitched across it in hot pink writing.

'Get him whatever he wants,' says Alejandro.

'But the bus,' says the youngish man.

'Fuck the bus,' says Alejandro. Zen is eating just to eat. He lifts the fork to his mouth. 'I'm going there too. I'll take you.'

Viewed side-on, the youngish man does not look unfamiliar. His blazer's faded at the shoulders, and so is the piping along his black denim. Alejandro squints, waiting for the familiarity to calcify into something more solid, but nothing comes. He taps his cup at the old woman crossing before them, ferrying another tray to another table.

'Poor satellite,' says the youngish man, stretching. 'Landing there.'

'Ideal, in a way,' says Alejandro, sawing a fried egg in half with the blade of his fork. 'If a satellite hit Coatzacoalcos, right? I'm not sure anyone could tell.'

'It is a remarkable shithole,' says the youngish man, head back, scratching under his chin, his nails making a noise on the stubble.

'Space shit is cool,' says Alejandro. He mixes the yolk with the sauce. 'There was a meteoroid, last year.'

'Above Ecatepec,' says the youngish man.

'Yes,' says Alejandro. 'It pancaked in the air above Ecatepec, showered blistering dust over rooftops and car-bonnets, hurt nobody.'

'Lucky,' the youngish man says, 'like the Tunguska fireball, a two-hundred-foot lump of rock and ice bursting half a dozen miles above the earth, smashed hundreds of kilometres of Siberian taiga to matchsticks, a few hours later and it would have been over St Petersburg and destroyed the whole city.'

'It's mad how nobody's died of a space rock,' Alejandro says.

The youngish man wags his finger, says, 'A dog in Egypt in 1911. Space pumice. Like the chunk that hit a Ugandan boy on the shoulder in 1992. All he heard was a whistle, like a kettle boiling, then a thud knocked him right over.'

Alejandro gets a shiver, thinking what might have happened if that rock had struck the kid's head.

'That's mental,' he says.

'You never hear the one that kills you,' says the youngish man, his eyes shut, his hands crossed on his chest.

'It'd be cool to get killed by a thing falling from space,' says Alejandro. He balls up his napkin, drops it on the mess on his plate. 'Those quesadillas are taking a while.'

'Should we just—' says the youngish man, with a bob of the head towards the door.

'I think so too,' says Alejandro, pulling bills from the wad, leaving them on the table. He points to the youngish man's cup. 'You going to drink that?'

He shakes his head and Alejandro drains the cup – they go outside into the building wind, and climb onto the bike. His grip's chilly even through the biker leathers, and

Alejandro's glad that he has his helmet on: the smell he's giving off is like ashtrays under dirty rain. But then he's able to pick up speed on the motorbike, and the bike wind blows it all to rags.

'You think we'll see anything?' shouts the youngish man into his ear. There's a buzz around his words from the mic in his helmet. 'When the satellite hits?'

Alejandro squints at the fog, says, 'A flash. Maximum.'

'Then nothing,' the youngish man says.

'We like nothing,' says Alejandro.

'Oh, yes,' says the youngish man, patting Alejandro's hips. 'Yes, we do.'

A few hours later, Alejandro stands in a hotel restaurant beside the youngish man. They're watching the storm crash against the windows, contrary to all predictions of the weather app. Alejandro wants to punch out the window he's so mad. He won't be able to see shit through these clouds – maybe hear the boom of the satellite, nothing else.

'Could be worse,' says the youngish man.

'How?' says Alejandro.

Rain and spray dash the panes. Hefty police speedboats cruise back and forth across the bay, their blue lights winking. From the pier hangs a black-and-red sign calling the state government murderers and thieves.

'I'm not sure,' says the youngish man.

Alejandro goes and sits in a booth. He pours coffee from a Thermos and takes the chocolate cake in its

Tupperware from the bag at his feet and sets it between them and pops off the lid.

'Go on,' says Alejandro, handing the youngish man the spoon from his coffee saucer. 'Have a divot.'

'Well, I don't think I can, chief,' the youngish man says, spreading his hands. The stitches holding his hands to his wrists are unignorable now. The grave smell rises. Alejandro swallows a tart bead of bile.

'And why's that?' he says in a voice that even he can hear is tight.

'My stomach's in a jar,' says the youngish man, 'back behind you. In UNAM.'

Alejandro's spoon hovers in the air. His throat tightens. For a moment, he pictures himself from outside – a lone, heavyset man in a pristine booth, an image that gives nothing away, like the advertising billboard outside his apartment – which is when the waiter sidles up and pours out more coffee and Alejandro, alone again, blinks and breathes the air in the restaurant – lemon floor cleaner, burned coffee, chocolate cake, safe smells, hotel smells.

'How long will this storm last?' Alejandro says to the waiter. He watches the waiter bob the Thermos. He watches the stream braid, unbraid. Laminar flow, they called it on Discovery.

The waiter looks out through the huge bay window, clicks his tongue like he's only just realised it's raining, and says, 'Oh, a while, I'd say,' before going to stand by the door to the restaurant.

Alejandro sits with his elbows propped on the table and his nose and mouth pressed against his clasped hands. He won't see shit. What was the fucking point Jesus fucking Christ what was the fucking point. On the wall hangs a framed sepia photo of a young boy in linen trousers, a tilma, and a straw hat, the sea glimmering behind him. His pose is slack and zombified from standing so long for the old-style camera. An enormous snake lies dead beside him, so big that the boy's head doesn't clear its dead eye, a soaked, dirty collar of feathers covering half its body.

Teresa messages: she and Sandra are praying for rain, the swelter there is unbearable and the pollution so bad her photo of their window looks like drifts of mustard gas.

'Swap,' Alejandro replies, with a photo of his rain-crawled window and then starts eating again, trying to flatten the panic in his belly. The waiter returns with a second coffee refill.

'Is that picture real?' Alejandro asks.

'Of course,' says the waiter, without looking. 'This town was full of snakes before they built the waterfront. Fat ones, thin ones, hairy ones. Sometimes there'd be a river of snakes flowing through the grass. You'd have to wait for all of them to pass before you could keep walking.' He finishes pouring with a flourish. 'But that one was the biggest they ever found. That's the owner's grandfather in the picture.'

The waiter gets his phone out and shows Alejandro a photo of a metal sign holed with rust. 'That's why it's called "Coatzacoalcos", see?' The sign shows the verse from Isaiah that he knows from the prayer services: '*The nursing child shall play by the cobra's hole, And the weaned child shall put his hand in the viper's den*', but with the word COATZACOALCOS written in Gothic blackletter instead of the last two words.

'Want anything else?' the waiter says. 'Beer or something?'

'I'm retired,' Alejandro says. 'Sparkling water.'

'Alrighty then,' the waiter says, sliding away from the booth, and Alejandro swaps to the seat on the other side, his back to the photo and to the sea.

The storm abates enough for Alejandro to risk the hotel pool. Wind has blown a dead crab right up to the door, and he kicks it out of his way, hearing it smush on the gravel. It looks the way his hand did the last night he drank. He remembers waking to the cratered plaster of his walls, holding a tan horn of his own shit bagged in his underwear, chew-marks on the turd. He's fine now, though. Goes to meetings and everything, keeping an eye out for the jittering leg, the nibbled lips, the fake nods, hooking them afterwards for a coffee or some tacos, so they can vent with him instead of relapsing like he did, even sponsors a girl about to move to Chihuahua with her boyfriend.

But right now, he has a feverishness he tries to tell himself is just the cold, even though its cloy reminds him of the youngish man. It's the neediness of ghosts that gets him, that unhoused feeling off them, like the soul leaves the body and then goes nowhere. It must suck to be a ghost. It must really suck.

The rain's a cooling sprink of drops on his forehead. The app tracking the satellite shows a zoomed-in view of the isthmus. The clouds are still so thick it doesn't matter how close it is.

He pulls off his Cruz Azul jersey and drops it on the pool chair, slides his feet out of their flip-flops, heads for the water. The pool's all his here, he never gets to use the one on his roof, weekends are unbearable with barbecues and Bluetooth speakers and normie cunts and the questions about his wife, how she is, where she is, is he alright after it all, they can all fuck off. He jogs through the drench, rain bullet-hard against his skin, his feet slapping the concrete, then launches himself into a deep whooshing swoop through the water, a great sea-noise blooming around him, and then the cool of it belts him full in the chest. He ploughs into his lengths, rain on his head, a rumble of water on water that kills the din in his head.

Afterwards, Alejandro leans back against the rim of the pool in the roar of the storm. He sucks in the smell of rain on hot concrete, the water running down his face and beard like he's in a film, in an ad.

There's a lulling gargle from the pipes and gutters, and then there it is: the whoosh, the bang. His eyes open and above him a great white scar pulls itself across the sky. The flare widens, trailing white cottony incandescences that taper down off its central line. He feels a nick of disappointment and he hears the youngish man again: *You never hear the one that kills you.* Then the debris comes down: clunk and tunk and clang, the smell of plastic, the hiss of burning. Underwater, he imagines the lounge chair shorn in two, an umbrella singeing. But coming up, he finds no space trash has killed him, he's still stuck here, with it all, the time in the sandy nowhere outside Juárez, tussocks as stiff and black as nets in the headlights, the truck wobbling down the bare track, bumping knees against other men, the buckles of their rifle-straps against the muzzles, the stocks squeaking grit against the metal floor, green and red and white arches of light in the distance, his gut clenched as hard as a billiard-ball as the truck passes through the blare of cumbia and reggaetón, laughter from windows and back gardens, the Canelo fight, until they pull in at the Sangre de Cristo rehab shelter and the crack of a shot craters the nightwatchman's forehead – the chief wanted it to look like narcos did it so he shoots him a few more times – loosely, though, no double-taps, then slinks with the others from game room to TV room, via the breezeblocks and rusted spigots in the former Pemex canteen where the addicts write their testimonies, then out to the dorms, most of them too sleepy with meds or methadone to scream or run all that much, and besides, his earplugs do for the rest of the noise, so it's point and pop, backs and necks and navels and throats appearing in the white flare of his torch, and he empties the whole magazine into one kid who's lying in bed with his headphones on, his book spread on his chest like a bird, letters showing through the torn gap in the cover, the missing '*Pe*' in *Pedro Páramo* re-inked in shaded-in ballpoint on the page beneath, skeletons in their Sunday best on the cover, lowering a coffin into a dry-looking grave. A suck and a rattle like a blocked drain rises from the kid's burst throat.

Alejandro lies sprawled in the water, the hail pelting down around him like the debris of the Chinese satellite. It's almost as though there really had been one. He feels himself kick in sleep and gives a start. He drifts any longer he might drown. He swims for the edge, muscles tingling with the long swim, and pulls himself up, catches the hailstones full on the chest. He stands there, eyes shut and arms out to feel as much of them as possible, their tink, their patter. These scenes from a film he feels he can curl up inside. He hears voices above and behind him: people standing at their windows, saying, 'Wow', 'What the hell', 'Amazing'. One floor below, someone starts clapping, but then a woman says, 'Hail can't hear you, Pablo', and the clapping stops.

It's not going to happen, Alejandro thinks to himself, and this time the disappointment is a fibrey breakage, almost a gentleness. He dries himself and he feels ridiculous and overfed, but whatever – at least he's not a ghost. White hail pelts his skull, the sting enough to kill any thought, leaving him here and only here, now and only now, towelling himself just to towel himself, nothing more, no one there, just him alone in the world's molecular helter baring itself all around him, a mell of white hail and high wind in the gathering dark.

BETTER

Diego didn't realise the quake was happening until it was over. Standing up from the midmorning lines at the table, head back, rolling his shoulders and midriff like it might shake more powder out of his sinuses, he counted to eight, waiting for the ignition, when the sudden rugby-tackle belt of the quake made him think for a second that he'd gotten lucky on a strong line, until he'd seen the swaying of the bike-chain chandelier above his head, the one his ex hadn't taken with her when she'd left a week ago now.

He waited, steadied himself against the table, watching his ex's cat, Piaf, stay right where she was. It was Diego's first big quake. He was from Aguascalientes: this kind of thing doesn't happen there. But animals are supposed to be clever in these situations he had heard, so – as the apartment shunted, the rhythm sexual, obscene – he also did nothing, just dabbed at the last of his lines from the mirrored tray and rubbed his gums, braced against the shaking and waiting for it to stop: or, at least, for the shaking to go back to normal, because he's never really not shaking, is he, not anymore, either with comedown shivers or with the feeling that his nerves are about to writhe and wriggle out of his skin with the electric joy of whatever he's managed to get hold of – heroin, ideally, but coke would do, or speed, or 2CB.

The shaking stopped.

Piaf went back to clapping her paws at the fruit-flies by the bin. He went back to bed, got lost in the warm golden spins, and eventually slept – until this voice, the one from outside the apartment door, came butting through his skull like the edge of a shovel, calling, 'Hello? This is Civil Protection! Anyone here?'

The liquid thrum of his own high is gone now. He's ironing-board rigid in the bed, and cold.

The Civil Protection voice huffs out a heavy sigh, tuts, and says, 'OK, look, if there's anyone there, we're obliged to let you know that this building has been deemed unsafe, and you're advised to leave as a precaution. OK? But we're not going to drag you out.'

Unsafe? This makes him sit up. A bowling-ball of pain rolls to the front of his skull. He has to lie down again, his eyes shut against its spreading white star. It really doesn't last as long as it used to, the heroin.

He slides from his bed, clatters into his bong, cracks it, hears the big glug of the stagnant water as the slick of guck and tar and dead flies seep across the tiles. Stepping back from the tide of seepage, his heel knocks an open bottle of Sancerre Edmond Vatan that he kneels to steady.

He creeps from the bedroom into the combination sitting-room and kitchen, the white laboratorial tiles greyed with dust and caught hairs. He moves towards the door that leads to the corridor. Echoing up the stairs he hears his building manager's voz de pito, and the hairs of his neck stand up so quick he expects them to tingle. They must just want rent, he thinks. Tomorrow's the nineteenth.

The door begins to open. Alarm ripples through him. He pastes himself to the wall side, grips it with his fingers to keep himself flat against it, out of sight in the slim space behind the door. He hears the drift of broken glasses scrape across the floor. He's been draining them and chucking them against the door. It makes the cat scamper around with fear. He likes scaring that little fucker.

'We're coming in,' says the Civil Protection voice.

'Oh Jesus,' says a third voice. All three are inside his apartment now.

'That's not quake damage,' the building manager says. Just in front of him, through the gap between the hinges, he sees her adjust the auburn mane of her hair. Her perfume smells like gardenias, but stirred into bin-smell, powder-smell, drink-smell. 'He just lives that way.'

'Right, well, *I* didn't know that,' says the Civil Protection voice. Diego can see him now: a hefty guy around his own age, in jeans and loafers and the regulation orange chaleco, his half-rimmed glasses pristine, his hair shining in spikes of hair-gel.

43

'Need a new Richter scale for that kind of chaos.'

He laughs at his own joke. Diego wants to hit him with the hammer he keeps in the cupboard. It's not his fault. Things are just too slippery to grip these days.

There's the Civil Protection guy, the building manager, and now a short, skinny cop, who sneezes and says, 'Ah fuck, is there a fucking cat in here?'

'Better not be,' said the landlord, hands on her hips, clopping around the kitchen table in her chunky heels. Now and again she pauses to inch around some debris, and her steps echo in the emptiness: Diego's ex, Anabelle, took her share of the furniture – which is to say, all of the furniture – when she left the week before. Diego looks at his own fingers trembling against the flat of the wall. He has no idea what they'll find in here. He has no idea what there is. Not much of it is legal, though, that's for sure. And that's before he gets to how much rent he's behind on. The bills – water, electricity, internet – have piled up and greyed under the door like shot gulls. The landlord runs a finger along what's left of the bathroom door. Diego's been punching it. All that's left is a big, Brazil-shaped chunk of chipboard with the door-handle still in it. She clicks her tongue.

The cop says, 'Well, look, you want me to go looking for hash or crack or heroin in this motherfucker's sock-drawer, this is not the fucking night for that, OK? Just check he's alive and we're gone.' He sneezes again. 'Jesus. He *has* got a cat in here. Cunt.'

'If there's a cat in here,' the building manager says, and doesn't complete the threat.

'He'll lose his deposit?' The Civil Protection guy laughs, then gestures at the room. 'Well, I've got news for—'

There's a big shunt, like a huge foot coming down, and everything lurches. The building manager yelps and grabs the faux-marble sideboard, the cop says, 'Jesus', and the Civil Protection guy just narrows his eyes and squints at the jagged 'V'-shaped crack in the ceiling, like he's trying to stop the aftershock with his mind.

'I don't care if this cunt is El Chapo,' says the cop, and sniffs. 'I'm not going looking for kilos just so's you can kick him out. Find some other cunt. I'll be sneezing for days after this.'

'If you make it down the stairs,' says the building manager.

'Do not jinx this.' Diego watches the cop wag his finger. 'This is not the ship I want to go down with.'

'Not luxe enough for you?' says the building manager, less aggrieved than tired.

The Civil Protection guy squints at the ceiling and says, 'Oh, I don't know, I think it will hold up another hour or so. If we don't get another one.'

The cop goggles at him. The Civil Protection guy gives a glassy smile.

'That's fine,' says the building manager. 'If it's still standing, we'll kick the fucker out. If he's still alive. If he's dead it's just a different set of papers.'

'Junkies,' says the cop.

Diego feels his grip about to come loose from the wall, then feels himself come loose entirely, just as the Civil Protection guy approaches the door, the way you're most likely to piss your pants right when you get home, no matter how long you've held on to it during the bus trip or whatever.

The building manager follows the Civil Protection guy and Diego falls forward against the door as it closes, and the slam of it is so loud he hears the cop yelp in the hallway. He lies there panting for a moment, eyes shut, listening to the clop of the building manager's high heels recede down the hall. Diego leans down to the hinges and peeks through the gap.

The corridor is totalled, plaster fallen from the ceiling, wires toppled through like vines. Across the hall, he can see into the apartment owned by that fisherman with the corkscrew curls and frequent recurrences of malaria, the one who's always filing noise complaints. He sees the cop shrug, the Civil Protection guy tut, the building manager put her hand to her mouth.

Lying amid splintered furniture and heaped glass Diego sees a covered shape on the ground. There's a damson stain at its head. Diego hears the shock of his own breath, and he falls forward against the door. The wall will hold him up, surely, he thinks, though maybe all bets are off. He palms and palms across the floor towards the bottle of Sancerre, grabs and slugs: out-all-night, appley stalor. Weather's gone to sleet and fog the last few days so it's still cold.

That sailor can't be the only one. There'll be other bodies nearby now: dead ones. The bottle to his lips, he drinks, drains, watches a collar of bubbles slide breaking down the neck and past the shoulder, then lets the bottle shatter to the ground, because it's not like he's sticking around, and it's not like his deposit's coming back to him, either. He reaches into the pocket of his bathrobe, checks his phone. There's no signal. He goes to the balcony, parts the blinds with his fingers; helicopter lights ticking back and forth through the soaked evening dark. His building is still up. So's every other one around. But there aren't any cars parked out front anymore, and a bunch of fences over the building-site are buckled and toppled. Then there's a sizzle, and all the lights die except for the blue glow of his laptop open on the couch.

He picks up and relights the joint he has left on the rim of the ashtray. If he's going to get out of here he's going to need to be as numb as possible: no way he's going past that body in the corridor without too much of something in his system.

A mewl reaches him through the door to the balcony. Next comes the thud of a tiny headbutt against the glass. Piaf scratches the glass, the sound like metal spikes turning in his head.

'Alright, alright,' he says, whipping open the door. If he knew how close a call she'd had with the cop and the building manager she wouldn't be whining like this.

She scampers in, stops, her eyes huge, her body braced, fixing to spring away from him if she has to. She looks a lot like Anabelle did towards the end: stung, flinching, tiny hands to her face.

He opens the cupboard and from within tin cans and a hammer tip thunder out over him. A metal head clunks against his knee. As he bends, yowling, a tin can catches him full in the forehead. Another star of pain flashes so hard and bright through his skull that he tips backwards, knocks yesterday's mug, the sugar bowl, a cognac bottle in a long sheeting avalanche to the floor.

He lands winded on the floor, head-level with the crate of luxury wines Anabelle left behind, some scheme of Ramses' who'd stolen them from his parents' cellar. He'd brought them over, sweaty, triumphant, plucking his stupid fucking goatee, his hands shaking too much to light his cigarette, rattling off dollar-prices, 'That Sancerre right there, that's three hundred bucks,' and the tired way Anabelle had said, 'that's great, baby,' from the couch. The last time he and Anabelle had sex, they had it on that couch, just after they'd got it, before they'd even unwrapped the thing. That's a while ago now. And he didn't feel much. Most of the want came from the buzz of that high-sativa half-joint they'd smoked in order to steel themselves for lifting the couch. Lying on the floor, he watches the helicopters hovering over the building sites.

Piaf circles amid the tumbled cans. There's no opener. That's why the hammer. He has to drive a knife into the tin with it and follow it all the way around. Piaf pushes a can with her paw and mews. How long's it going to be, he thinks, before the body across the way's going to begin smelling: and what's going to be in that smell that might kill you, might spread black spores through your lungs. Unless he gets down deep enough in sleep he can swim under the time between now and the dead guy's relatives or somebody comes for him. And for that he's going to need heavier duty sleep. And for that he's going to need to get himself inside again, inside with the needle.

He collects the needle, holds it up, pricks his finger against it, contemplates the length of it, so dirty, so thin, so black. Absently, he circles the top of the needle's plunger with his thumb while his other hand pulls the belt from the loops of his dressing gown – he puts one end between his teeth while the other pulls it tight around his forearm.

The doorbell rings.

Diego turns, lifting the needle, ready to stab.

'Dude?' a voice says through the door.

The belt drops from between his teeth. Piaf climbs up his arm to his shoulder.

'C'mon, bro – I can see the light under the door. You in there?'

Diego knows this voice, too: Adonai. Since he's survived an overdose he's found God, gotten clean, and been running a chilaquiles place with his girlfriend. Diego tied off one night drunk, fell asleep, woke up without the feeling in the fingers of his right hand and had to quit playing guitar. And even though his best work, to be fair, had already been well behind him by then; 'like an orchestra struck by lightning', a reviewer in *TimeOut México* said and, while those hacks can go fuck themselves, of course, Diego's bones still hum with the power of that sound, and his arms ache after the red weight of his Gibson, after how long it took to pay for that guitar, all those kitchen-hours and grease-marks on the backs of his hands.

The doorbell rings again.

'Fuck, dude,' yells Adonai. 'Just let me know if you're alive in there.'

Diego sighs. He takes a corkscrew from the table, pops open a Châteauneuf du Pape, and takes a long, slow belt of it, slowing the rolling of the headache around his skull, before crossing the room to open the door.

Adonai bursts through, seizing him in a bear-hug, saying, 'Oh, man, I'm so glad.'

He rocks a little, swaying Diego against him, and Diego feels his hand pat the back of his skull. Piaf watches Adonai from under the countertop. Well over six foot, and tattooed from his shaved head all the way down, Adonai looks a lot scarier than he is. Some have a prison vibe – swallows and cobwebs, a cross beside his actual eye for a cellmate he saw get stabbed to death in front of him – on his neck Jamaica flags and Ras Tafari staffs and all sorts. When Adonai lets go, he blows out a heavy breath, shaking his head. 'Thank God, man,' he says. 'Just thank God.'

He steps past Diego into the room. The floor crunches under his feet.

'There's, like, thousands of people missing, man. And, like, this neighbourhood, yeah? It's a trending topic, or whatever. Account of all the dead folks.'

Diego's gaze creeps towards the door, towards the dead fisherman across the hall.

'How many we talking?' he says.

Adonai's hand flaps the air. 'Like un chingo, wey, no sabes. This one place in Portales went up, like, fuck, you know? Like it was smoke. Saw it on the news.'

Diego's foot taps the floor. 'Everyone we know OK?'

Adonai shrugs. 'Only started checking. But fuck, man, it is creepy in that hall. Lights out. No sound. Think this place has about ten minutes left in it.'

As Adonai says this, Diego feels the shunting beneath his arse begin again, Adonai watching the sway of the chandelier, and a long, cold phlegm blob of fear drops languorously through his body. Piaf slinks out from under the countertop and settles beside Adonai. He watches the chandelier go still, then begins to pet her.

'And Anabelle, everything like that?' he says.

'Gone,' says Diego, fixing his dressing-gown so his balls don't show. He scratches his cheek. 'A week? I don't know.' He looks at the cognac bottle and feels anger boil in his chest as there's no discreet way to tip it into his cup.

Adonai sucks his teeth. 'Shit. And you'll stay here?'

'Depends,' says Diego, swirling his cup.

'On?'

'What do you think?' He spreads his arms up. 'On the fucking structural integrity of the building, yeah?'

'Alright, man, whatever.' Adonai gives a one-shoulder shrug, sighs, and says, 'But, you know, mostly I swung by to take you somewhere.'

'Forgive me, but, well, a man of your' – he flaps a hand in Adonai's direction – '*vibe*, let's say, being vague about where he might, ah, *relocate* me – how do I put this?' but he gives up: 'Ah, man,' he says eventually, 'words are really hard for me, you know?'

Adonai lets out a rippling laugh and says, 'Bro, c'mon, you think I can't tell?' He gives a chin-jut at Diego's arm.

For a burning second Diego wants to take up a handful of shards from the floor, cut out that bruise, scrawl away the trackmarks on his arms.

'Hell, chief. No judgement or whatever.'

'I don't want to stop,' Diego says. 'It's all I'm good at. It's a real talent. Not a lot of people.' He crosses the other leg the other way, remembers the ballhang, presses his gown to himself. 'You know. Make a priority. Of that.'

'Only goes one way, man.' Adonai frowns, sucks his teeth. 'Deathwards. And, I mean, you know, not like you get too far away from that at the best of the times either. Day like today… this, like, quake split the gas mains open on my street,' he says. 'Nobody realised it even happened. Smell was there, yeah, but we assumed it was pretty far, because it was kind of faint. When the shakes end, we're all, like, hugging, crying. And one of the neighbours takes a couple of steps away, lights a cigarette. Blooms into flame where he's standing. Survives the quake by literally four seconds,' Adonai says. 'And that's it. His yells sounded so upset. Wailing like how unfair it all was.'

Diego says nothing.

'You're a lucky guy, man,' Adonai says. 'You're a lucky, lucky guy.' He reaches across to Diego, grips his shoulder, holds his gaze, and says, 'I wouldn't want to move either. Moving's tiring. Specially when you're fucked up or whatever.' His gaze creeps to the chandelier again. It hasn't moved.

'Could make you some food, round my place. No biggie.'

Adonai claps his hands together, louder this time.

'Can I think about it?' Diego tries to say, but the noise out of him sounds like a door creaking open.

Adonai says, 'Remember how you had an itch above your appendix and decided it was bowel cancer? And the heart attack that turned out to be a panic attack? Well, brother, you know, this time? Maybe you're right to be worried.'

Diego sucks down a drag of smoke.

'You want to hit the sack, yeah?' Adonai says. He stands up, crosses the room, and gives Diego a pat on the shoulder. 'No problem. I'll sleep on this couch, make sure you're OK.'

Diego nods.

'OK.'

Adonai slips away through the door. There's a clink of bottles being gathered. While he's in there, Diego reaches for the shoebox under the couch, lifts off the lid. He holds the spoon and the revolver-shaped blowtorch-lighter that Anabelle brought him from Prague. He hears the soft roar of the blue flame, the bubble and seethe of the heroin-sliver melting, the creep of the smoke as thick and rich as a slow bassline. The needle's there, too, half-hidden by balled-up tissues spotted with blood. He imagines picking it up, though the very thought of it sends a wave of weary nausea over him, and so, when he hears Adonai suddenly behind him saying, 'Want me to collect that, too?' he just says, 'Yeah, sure', and lets Adonai lift the box from his hands with the tiniest of sifting noises, cardboard brushing skin.

'Sweet,' Adonai says, and carries it over to the bin. 'You got a spare blanket for a brother?'

'Uh.'

Adonai laughs, waves a hand at the air. 'Nah. I'll call my girlfriend, tell her where I'm at.'

Diego nods and gets to his feet. 'And she won't mind?'

Adonai hauls the box wines in from the balcony and says, 'She does this shit, too, man – it's all good.'

'Alright. Well, thanks, man.'

Diego heads to the bedroom, and is about to topple into the bed's big white marshmallow when an aftershock shakes the light. Diego peers up at the ceiling, waiting for it to open, no fear in him at last. But nothing happens. He lets himself fall, which feels almost like a lifting, the warmth of two arms lifting him up, or something like that, perhaps – but then he's gone, and can't be sure of anything anymore.

CLEANER

Lucio's wife and daughter are asleep upstairs and he is nodding off in front of *Heat* – alone on the couch where he sleeps – when his daughter's teacher, Yael, texts him for the first time since she ended their affair.

Hey, are you busy?

He doesn't know what to tell her. The thrill of her name on the screen dies immediately. He's been happily settled on the couch, the crick in his back slowly loosening, even thinking of having a bowl of his daughter's Coco Pops, if there are enough in the box.

Hi, he says. *Long time.*

Hi, yeah. Listen. Sorry. Little emergency.

On the screen, a black tar of burst eardrum leaks from the side of a dazed-looking bank guard's head. Michael Mann really did his homework on this film. The steam rising from the bullet-holes in Robert De Niro's chest, the thing about eyeballs turning black when people are shot in the head – he loves these bits. Nobody cares enough about bodies to know things like this. But Michael Mann does. If they met, he thinks they'd get on, talk about stuff. Lucio's a forensic cleaner, sterilising the homes of people who've been murdered, or died of neglect, or become hoarders. One dead hoarder's house can stink up a whole street.

The cursor pulses at the bottom of the WhatsApp window on Lucio's phone. While he is trying to pick words out of the big wad of everything he's never been able to say to Yael, she calls him.

'Are you there?' says Yael.

'Little?' he says. 'Little emergency? How's that?'

'My. Oh, look. It's someone I know. I think he's overdosed.'

'Where?' Lucio turns off the TV, kicks back the blanket, wedges the phone between his cheek and his shoulder, and takes his black slacks from where they're sitting folded on the armchair.

'My place.'

'OK,' Lucio says, pulling on the trousers, standing into his Florsheim penny loafers, the ones that look like silencers but with buckles on. He tells himself he's not dropping everything for her: he's only doing this because the Twelfth Step says to carry the message to the addict who still suffers. But he can't pretend – as he checks in his briefcase for the little thing of naloxone that he always carries – that he doesn't also love the excuse to get out of here, that the air in the house at night hasn't been too hot and tight since Claudia gave him another chance.

'I'll be there in ten minutes,' he says to Yael, then hangs up before she can thank him. He's groggy, his nose stings;

at the end of every job he has to drop a bomb of sulphides and nitrites to chase out whatever airborne particles of dirt and blood and interior-body bacteria there might be hovering in the air. Even with the ventilator on, something of that bomb always gets through the mask. Today's was a big job, the biggest all year – eight people, stabbed to death at a house in Colonia del Valle. Every spatter, every tear in the curtains, every dragging handprint along the paint and the plaster, he saw in his head as a scream, a jetting artery, shock-widened eyes. It was a long job.

The sting is as much in his head as anything, because with all of the time he spends mixing his formulas – titrating, calibrating, thinking in millilitres and milligrams and parts-per-million – he feels like nothing but a person-shaped cloud of atoms moving through a bigger cloud of atoms.

He's out the door and over to the car. Their dog, Lucinda, is still up, pacing the garden. She's a rust-coloured barrel-chested mastiff, and she's been barking a lot at night. He blows her a kiss and gets into the car. She watches him, tail down, looking worried.

His daughter, Natalia, is only six and reads everything she can find. Which means she is bored by almost everything else in class. She lays her head on her wrists face-down on the desk, banging her head and groaning gently whenever they are doing maths or anything that involves drawing. That changed when Yael had come along. Lucio went to thank Yael after class one day and ask her how she'd done it. He was surprised she was so young – maybe twenty-six, twenty-seven – her arms tattooed with the same futuristic, red-and-black things as the streaks in her hair. She was courteous, cool, professional.

'I give her older kids' readers,' she said, taking a book that showed an old man and an old woman slowly turning into two trees knitted together by their branches. He flicked through the pages, saw boxes, English words, French ones.

'It's for fourteen-year-olds, that one,' Yael said. 'And we're compiling this.'

She took out an A4 notebook with a seamed green cover and handed it to him. Lucio ran a finger along the cracks.

'It's her dictionary. Every time she doesn't get a word,' Yael said, 'she writes down the definition in here.'

Lucio moved through the pages, turning them gently. The new words in red, the definitions in blue, the cursive so careful that the letters could be diagrams of veins and arteries. This was why Natalia's so calm now. This was why he could sit beside her playing chess on the computer while she did her homework.

'Joined up writing,' he said.

Yael shrugged. 'It's not easy when something isn't clicking. I don't want that for her. I lost a whole summer because I couldn't figure it out. My father held me back. Watching my cousins play with SuperSoakers and there I was, trying to get the "S" to go right.'

Lucio tugged his earlobe, looking at the stack of pages on the table.

'You really do give a shit don't you,' he said.

'I don't know. The bar is low for that. At least in this school.'

'I think it's OK. It keeps people safe.'

'That's what I mean,' said Yael.

Lucio thought of the MISSING poster on the lamppost he'd walked past: a fat kid, holding his neck like he was trying to hide how fat he was, a nervous smile on his face.

'I see kids doing dangerous stuff and their parents don't even notice,' said Yael. She winced and put her hands on her hips. 'And when I try to say something, I get the Riot Act over it. So it's nice to. I don't know. Have this.'

'Have what?'

'A conversation where I'm not pushing at a closed door.'

'Well,' said Lucio. 'Let's make a plan for her then.'

'How do I get hold of you?'

He fumbled his business card out of his wallet for her then, the thing jogging over his fingers like he was getting a condom out of the wrapper.

She squinted at the description.

'It's not morbid,' said Lucio. 'Before you say anything.'

'Well, I didn't think it was,' said Yael. 'Same kind of thing we do here isn't it.' She whapped the card against the second knuckle of her index finger. 'I get to ask how you got into it?'

'When we have more time, maybe,' he said.

He saw her for a stilted coffee at a place he'd felt too young to be in – to discuss Natalia, they'd said. Yael had made a real plan: reading lists of Greek myths, little formats where Natalia could write police reports on monsters from programs and games that scared her. Feeling a swell of what Lucio had promised himself was just admiration, he put his hand on the inner fold of her arm. She'd just looked at him and said, 'So, do we have enough time to talk about your job, then?'

'We.' He looked at his watch. 'We might not.'

'Dinner, then,' she said.

He'd lied to his wife, Claudia, about a clean that had gone on longer than he'd expected.

It's foggy and dark. Across the road, the 'V's of the carpark lights at the Walmart look submerged. The blue glow of LEDs over a hot-dog stand and the bloody red and lush green of the Pemex blur into the same cool, lonely feeling. The lights inside Yael's house are cloudy, bluish, the outside painted a dirty mint, all of it so laboratorial. The house used to sadden him when they weren't having sex, the sickly jam-red half-gloom of her room, the slight choke in the throat he'd feel at those windows of hers that never let in enough light, but when the frenzy was on him it was like he was crashing through all notion of feeling, good or bad, those hard, bereft kisses of hers sucking him under into nothing, which was why he'd kept going back, until the grim wrench of the ending: chain-smoking on her doorstep all night, pressing the buzzer longer and longer, in a long insistent honk, in short chirrups he hoped might sound cheery, Independence Day fireworks crackling overhead, unable to leave because the speed-bump outside the building meant every car slowed and he'd get a leap and crash of hope thinking maybe it was the taxi bringing her back, staggering like a foal from its door into his hug – which got so bad he began to set limits to when he should give up hope: counting taxis, counting fireworks, finally just counting, then breaking all of the limits anyway, saying 'after thirty, after fifty, after a hundred', sure that if he waited he'd be rewarded and she'd take him in out of the cold, though it was only towards morning he went home, when she must have looked up from whoever she was with to reply to all his texts: *I'm celebrating with my mother. And I think your wife is right. We should maybe leave it. I've sort of met someone.*

He pulls up outside for the first time since that night, hearing the gravel crunch as he brakes. His thumb hovers over the buzzer, then presses it flat like he wants to drive it through the wall. Footsteps thunder down the stairs, there's a flash of dark hair in the window above the door, and then there she is, shorter than he remembers, pale, her eyes and mouth open in panic, and his mind vitrifies and shatters, leaving him with no room except to obey.

'I can't thank you enough,' she says, opening the door, the words coming out in a breath. She's in sweatpants and a striped t-shirt, looking tired and frantic. He feels the electric kick of her smell jolt up through him.

'Nothing to thank.' He clears his throat. 'And so? Where's the – you know.'

'Come on, come on,' she says, running back up the stairs.

Lucio shuts the door and goes up behind her, up towards a noise like a rasping saw. On the floor of the bathroom by Yael lies a young man gasping on his back on the tiles, his arms up and out in a 'Y'. He's wearing a mangy grey robe, the opening swagging so low that Lucio can see his small lilac nipples. A clear plastic tube is wrapped so tightly around his arm that the veins stand up high and blue. Lucio's owned dogs who looked heavier. Lucio walks over to him, lays a pair of fingers against the kid's throat. His pulse is going ninety, but it's strong.

'Good, good,' Lucio says, and sets down his briefcase. He opens the snaps, takes a clear vial of naloxone and a foil-wrapped syrette from the black foam lining inside, peels off the foil with a dainty scurry of his fingers. He slides the needle into the perforation in the jar and sucks up the liquid with a shallow, rasping snore. Stooping at Diego's side, he remembers Robert de Niro in *Heat*, all careful, frowning precision.

He taps the needle, then pulls back Diego's dressing-gown to jab him in the hip. Diego sits up with an angered grunt and Lucio hears Yael's shocked laugh of relief, sees the way she puts her hands to her mouth, and remembers he's just a chump with a beat-up Jetta. He's not even getting paid. Who will clean him up from everything when he dies?

'There we go,' Lucio says. The humiliation is shaking his entire body. He eases Diego back onto the floor with the flat of his palm. He hears his breathing already.

'You know, I think if we just turn him over and let him sleep it off, he'll be OK.'

'Let me.' Yael gets down on her hunkers as well, sending a waft of argan oil around him. She grips Diego by the hip and shoulder and slowly eases him onto his front, his forehead resting on the inner fold of his forearm. Diego's cheek kicks in response.

'You love him.'

'I don't want him to die, if that's what you mean.'

'That's a good start. He in a program or anything?'

Yael wavers her hand.

'He goes to meetings. He bounces in and out of there – slips, relapses.' She pulls a towel from the rail and lays it under Diego's head.

'There someone from the group you can call?' he says.

'I guess, yeah.' She reaches into Diego's dressing-gown pocket and swipes the screen unlocked.

'So you stayed an item,' Lucio says, watching her type. 'That's nice.'

'We *became* an item,' she says. 'We weren't anything when you and I finished.'

'Making me less than nothing, I suppose,' Lucio said.

'Don't be bitter.'

'Hey, I'm here, aren't I?'

'You're not being very nice.'

The phone buzzes.

'Sorry, one sec.'

She goes out. Lucio watches Diego's chest rise and fall. He could clasp his hand over Diego's nose and mouth until he went still. If he's pumping Diego's chest when Yael comes back, it'll look like the naloxone just didn't take. It happens all the time. A car scrapes past in the distance. A tang of woodsmoke cuts through the odour of raw sewage in the air.

Then Diego takes in a huge, sucking breath, his eyes startled wide, and sits bolt upright on the floor. Coughing, he says, 'Oh, Jesus. I thought I made it all the way that time. Oh man, it feels like I've a gallon of boiling paint in my head. What did you do to me?'

'Wasn't me.' Lucio gives another jerk of the head towards the bathroom door. 'Your girlfriend asked me.'

'That son-a-bitch,' Diego says dolefully in English, a cowboy twang to his voice.

Yael comes back upstairs.

'Adonai's on the way,' she says, as she enters the bathroom again. 'And I said I'd help a kid's mother with some forms. And it's just.' She lifts her hair up over her sticky-out 'Dumbo' ears. She starts again, 'It's just—'

'No problem,' he says. I'll sit with him till the sponsor's here.'

'You sure?' says Yael, but she's already moving her foot for the door. She always got like this about the kids, anyone who was even a little bit off.

'Woman on a mission,' says Lucio, and jerks his head. 'Go on.'

He hears her run up the hall and the bedroom door close.

Diego gets shakily to his feet, leaning on the toilet. Lucio puts an arm behind his shoulder. He could run his thumb along the long, shallow scallop of his scapular, he's that thin. Diego gives him a suspicious glower.

'You a doctor or what?'

Lucio shakes his head, easing him out the door, and starting down the stairs, which are wide enough for both of them.

'Cleaner,' he says.

'Why'd you have that injection shit on you, then?'

'My wife gets it for me.' They're all the way down the stairs now. 'She's a nurse.'

A dirty leer appears on Diego's face and he says, 'What, so my missus was your other woman, was it?'

'I thought,' says Lucio, 'that I was the other man.'

'Ow. Fuck. I've got pins and needles in my legs.'

'You passed out in a weird position. The feeling'll come back.'

Lucio leads Diego into the sitting-room, eases him down onto the couch. He turns on the TV, flips the channels. *Heat* is still on. Al Pacino is walking along the dry basin of a river, flapping his arms like a crow. Lucio pulls at the knees of his trousers as he sits down beside Diego.

'I come across a lot of ODs, cleaning,' Lucio says. 'Places I work tend to be pretty sad neighbourhoods.'

'Jesus.' Diego recoils a little. 'What kind of fucking cleaning do you do, man?'

Lucio can feel the marks of the ventilator mask on his face. He hates explaining his work. At the start, when he explained his job to cops, they'd frown at him, tell him they just got regular house cleaners in for that stuff. He'd walk back out under the police-station's throbbing fluorescents, his returned card in both hands, back out through the lilac glow of the vending machines in the waiting room where families dozed, feeling his body lose substance, feeling like an idiot. His hand claws his stomach and he watches Al Pacino say, 'He's good, this guy. Very, very good.'

'I clean up bodies,' Lucio says. 'I love it. And it's not morbid, before you say anything.'

Diego crosses his legs, flicks the robe to cover his thigh.

'Well, no shortage of work, anyway,' Diego says, after a moment.

'Two murders a week, I'm on,' he said.

Diego says nothing. On the screen, Val Kilmer is squinting at the moving blade of a tiny saw, a pale dust of metal silting up along its edge.

'Friend of mine – program guy – he's a murder detective. Tips me off,' Lucio says.

On the screen a helicopter is rising high over blurry canyons of yellow light, like it's lifting inside him.

'What I like about this film,' Lucio says, wagging his finger at the screen, 'is it's about two people who are so good at their jobs that they're bad at everything else.'

Diego frowns a little, then he nods, eases back against the sofa, says, 'Yeah.' Then he leans forward, holds his face in his hands, and says, 'Oh, man, I fucked up so much.'

'It's OK.'

'I had six whole months.'

'Yeah.'

'I don't know why she sticks around. I really don't.'

On the screen, Al Pacino is beating the shit out of a television.

'You don't need to say things like that,' Lucio says. 'She loves you. Better than that. She gets you.'

Diego flops back, his face all scrunched up. He's won, and he doesn't even realise it, but Lucio feels sad for the guy. It's always humiliating when someone has to take you back from the brink, when you're all set to leap and your steps stutter, the *Look what you made me do* dying in your throat. All you want is someone to coax you back, though you'd sooner cry than admit it. It's the sentimentality Lucio hates most about people in a relapse. They want an audience, not help.

Diego is looking at him with disgust.

'What?' says Lucio.

'Easy for you to say,' Diego says.

'What? Why?'

'You ever see yourself?'

'You've lost me.'

'Jesus.' Diego shakes his head. 'Nobody told you? Ever?'

'Told me what?'

Diego shakes his head. Robert De Niro is leant back against the banquette of a diner, scowling like a pissed-off teenager, Al Pacino staring at him manically.

'You're him,' Diego says, gesturing at the screen with both hands. The camera's just showing Robert De Niro now. Diego brushes his cheek with one finger. 'Your mole's just on the other side.'

'Huh,' says Lucio. The screen goes black before an ad-break. He sees himself reflected in the screen. For a moment it really is like the image of De Niro lingering there.

Diego tuts, shaking his head, and mutes the ads.

'Honestly, man, when you showed up, I thought I was hallucinating you. Thought Robert De Niro was taking me over the River fucking Styx, man.'

Lucio laughs.

'I'm not fucking laughing,' Diego says. 'Just like my fucking drug-attenuated interior life to see a fucking Dad-core film star showing up instead of saints and angels and shit.' He wags a finger. 'No, no. And that "Don't fuck with me look". You could melt pants at a hundred yards.'

He lifts the flap of his robe.

'Fuck, man, I'm on a semi here just describing it.' The naloxone hits some people funny, makes them manic. He hopes this Adonai guy arrives soon.

'I care that you're not dead. That's all.'

Diego snaps his fingers and points, saying, 'And *that*'s it. Right there. That's why I'm here with her and you're not.'

'Hey, now.'

'No. No. It's a compliment. She likes a project. A fixer-upper. And you're not that. You're all whole. I'm all hole.' He laughs a little. 'Probably you just looked a bit rumpled one day. And she thought that was you. But it was probably just a bad day.'

Lucio doesn't say anything. What relationship isn't founded on a misunderstanding, he wants to say to this kid. But what does he know. Though then the film comes back. He unmutes it. Diego keeps talking.

'This is what me and her are like, see,' he says, interlacing his fingers, pulling them taut. 'Compatible flaws, baby. Built to last. Till both of us dissolve.'

A yellow motorbike whizzes up to the door, slowing to a halt. A tall, heavyset man covered in tattoos gets off the saddle, doffing a helmet. He looks through the window with a worried expression and waves.

'Ah, shit,' Diego says. 'The fucking cavalry.'

'Great,' says Lucio, standing up with a deep breath. His chest feels tight and big at once. If he had to, he couldn't name the feeling. 'See you in a meeting, Diego.'

'Yeah, yeah.' Diego doesn't look away from the TV. 'Thanks.'

Lucio lets himself out, leaving the door ajar. The tall man – Adonai, he supposes – is coming up the path.

'Hey, man, thanks for that,' he says. He has crosses and teardrops under his eyes but the look on his face makes Lucio think of a golden retriever. 'How's our boy doing?'

'Nothing coffee and some food won't fix.'

Adonai shakes his head, looking through the window.

'I'd go through fire for that fucken idiot, man. Already went through a fucken quake for him, know'm saying? Like, literally, man.'

'He's got a certain charm,' Lucio says, looking in at the couch, where Diego's leg is up on the seat, tapping the cushion, while his mouth goes mauling at a hangnail. The lights of the shootout scene flicker over his face.

'Well, you know, you're welcome in our home group anytime, man. Be an honour. It's at 222 Insurgentes. Between the sex shop and the hipster pulquería.'

Adonai goes into the house. Lucio gets into his car and drives home. Morning light is coming up in the gaps between the clouds, the lurid magenta of candle-wax.

Day-labourers are gathering on the main street of Texcoco, faces seamed and ruddy with sun and work and boredom. The vans come earlier all the time, taking them away to build the new airport. They get out early from work and cause a ruckus, these men in their twenties, hanging around secondary schools, sometimes driving girls home in shared cars. Pasted to the side of the traffic-lights there's the MISSING poster of the chubby, smiling boy. Xerox copy-lines streak his face and hair. The note is mis-spelt, says that the kid is deaf, that he got separated from his mother in Walmart, could be anywhere. The lights change and Lucio goes the last seven blocks home.

When he gets home, Claudia is in the kitchen, battling with the coffee-filter.

'You went out,' she says.

'Yeah. I'm really sorry.'

'Work?' She slams the percolator against the wall and the filter-door stays shut. She flicks the switch. The spout begins to gutter. 'Oh fucking finally,' she says.

'Not work,' he says. 'Overdose. Nobody died.'

Lucio takes the foil wrap of the syrette from his pocket. He smooths it along the table. Claudia turns at the sound of the uncrumpling foil.

'I promise.'

She looks at the foil for a long time. Then she looks at his face and nods, smooths the foil flat, then begins to roll it back up along itself. She checks the time on her phone and says, 'This fucking machine. I don't leave now I'm late. You want to take Natalia to school?'

Lucio doesn't even ask if she's sure in case she withdraws the offer. It's been months. Sometimes they're both gone when he wakes up.

'Thanks,' he mutters, pockets the foil, and half-gallops up the stairs to Natalia's room.

Natalia is already sitting up when he gets to her room, her eyes wide, holding two fistfuls of blanket in a ball under her chin.

'Mama's mad,' she says, in a whisper.

'At the coffee-machine, love. Not at you.'

'Or you?'

'She'll be mad at me for a while yet.'

'I always say I'm sorry straight away when I do something wrong,' Natalia says. 'That works for me.'

'Thank you, love. I'll give that a try.'

Now Natalia purses her lips and lowers her chin further into the blankets, doing the Gizmo eyes.

'We don't even have Coco Pops, love,' Lucio says. 'I ate them.'

'Oh, well.' She sits up, shrugging, then tosses her hair, and swings her legs from the bed, suddenly a teenager.

'Get those teeth brushed and the uniform on like a good girl, will you?'

'And you'll let me pick the music in the car then, right?'

She looks at him over her shoulder, plucks a pair of tights from the drawer. The school they've put her in is a strict one, Catholic, but that uniform makes him wonder. They let you do what you want in the free ones, but at least every kid wears those beige tracksuits. Was that safer? Probably not, but they'll find out in the end, won't they, he thinks, as he shuts the door, goes down to the kitchen, and gets the Coco Pops out, because surprises drive Natalia wild altogether.

In the car, after breakfast, he watches her flutter her eyelids in the rearview mirror, eyes rolled up, like one of them from her TV shows.

'You get the second song.'

She leans forward, straining against her seatbelt, squints at the dashboard screen. 'Seven *minutes*?'

'The drum solo at the end,' Lucio says, pulling out of the driveway, 'is the pinnacle of Western popular music.'

'It sounds like music from inside an elevator,' Natalia says.

'If that was true,' Lucio says, 'I'd live in that fucking elevator. I'd take that elevator all the way to space.' He turns up the volume.

Natalia narrows her eyes at him.

'The "f"-word is twenty pesos.'

'Wow. It was less last week.'

'Pinned to the dollar. Watch the markets. I do.'

'What's my tab now?'

'Fifteen hundred.'

'Oh, what a coincidence,' Lucio says, stopped at the lights, wagging his finger for 'No' at the guy holding up a Coke-bottle of window-cleaner and a raggedy sponge. 'That's exactly how much school costs next term.'

At the school the security guard walks towards the curb, a shotgun held diagonal across his body, and leans towards the windscreen to check Lucio's face against the photo on his laminated information sheet. The school put him in after that thing in Tláhuac. The car stops. He kisses the air near his cheek.

He watches her as the knot of girls opens at her approach. A football arcs over Natalia's head, but she doesn't even look, just steps into her friends' hugs, a poised smile on her face. He has no idea where she got that from, but she's glad she has it. The ball skitters across the tarmac.

Lucio's car moves up the queue, level with the doorway, where Yael is leaning, her arms folded, her eyes ticking over the kids. She looks over at his car. She waves, but then stops herself. But that's enough for him, he supposes. He lifts a finger from the wheel, nods, then the car in front of him budges forwards enough for him to merge into the traffic that carries him away from her.

BEACH

Helena slows the car, pulls up at the beach, and gets out of the car. She's half-way into her cigarette when the storm hits. Under her umbrella, she listens to the drops puttering softly down around her, enjoying the metallic, pre-lightning sting and the sharp note of salt that rises from the dark lagging of dried seaweed on the shoreline. The rain is warm, long drops turning the sand brown to black.

Currents of water begin to rush out of the marram grass on the ridge above and behind where she's parked, growing on a bank of split rocks that make her think of dinosaur bones. Streams braid and wind over the floor of the arroyos around the lozenge of sand where she's parked. Everything is loud with salt-smell – the kelp, the emptied fish, the shells that have spilled out of a rip in a black plastic bag. The bag is heavy-duty, restaurant-issue, but no match for the gull tearing at it.

A wave comes in, swamping the restaurant bag, dousing the gull, who yawks and takes flight, and it's now that she begins to worry, because that tide's rising fast, and there's already a white fog rolling in from the sea up the sand

and suddenly everything further than two hundred yards is lost to the mist. The rushing sound in the arroyos has deepened, too, she notices, from a trilling sort of a splash to a glug, then a thunder, and now this flat roar. Dirty foam circles turn on the rising water. The edges of the sand that the car's on fizz and seethe and give way. A margin of bubbles starts to near her feet and her tyres. If she tries to drive now, she'd go bonnet-first into a wide flood.

'Fuck,' Helena says, biting at a hangnail, the cigarette burning out between the fingers of the other hand. Although she hugs the umbrella to herself, her forearms run with water, the force of the drops dimple her skin, a white vapour rising from her, runnels of water outlining the cross-hatch of old cuts up to the inner folds of her elbows, nearer to the good veins.

'Fuck,' she says again, and backs towards her car. She's been stupid. She's always stupid. This drive was stupid.

Her feet inch back from the shrinking edges of the sand. Helena tugs loose a hangnail between her teeth and feels a quick red zip of pain. Awakened now, she clamps the cigarette between her teeth, holds the umbrella to the side, and steps up onto the tyre. A sudden gust pulls the umbrella inside-out, lifting her backwards and though she yelps she doesn't lose grip and pulls herself up on the metal edge of the bonnet. She's standing up on it now but it's slippery: she drops to her knees, thunks her chin against the windscreen, hears the cigarette sizzle out in the wet, and with her fingertips pulls herself up the streaming metal, onto the roof where she lies there, gasping, the wind ballistic against the ragged umbrella.

The whole world beyond this little island of sand is lost. All she can see is four blinking red lights over at the far end of the bay, where the chimneys of a power plant pump out a garland of brown smoke that the rain weighs to the ground.

'Fuck,' she says again. 'Fuck, fuck, fuck.'

*

Leaving Mexico City it was just before the turn-off to the beach, beneath the reddish smoke, that she hit the first traffic jam. Part of a fence had buckled and pigs spilled out, their heads jockeying and craning as they jogged around the two lanes, sniffing at the cardboard boxes and sweet-wrappers, jumping when cars honked at them or nudged their rumps with their bumpers. One sow turned and squalled at the Mercedes that pushed her. Her stupid defiance, just like Helena's – released by the police just this morning and now this mad flight out of Mexico City.

She puts her head in her wet hands and groans. The umbrella slips. She doesn't even care, she's soaked anyway.

'Hello?' A voice shouting. She turns her head and sees a figure moving towards her through the rain. The wide tails of his hooded raincoat chase around his knees.

'You OK up there?' the voice says. It belongs to a man speaking Spanish, but with a heavy accent: United States, Canadian, who's to say.

'Uh, yeah,' she shouts back. 'Fine, fine.'

'Broken down?' He's an older man, maybe sixty or seventy, with a long grey beard that blows in the wind. His glasses are full of rain. He's wearing shorts and a pair of flip-flops, a heavy-looking toolbox hangs by his side.

'It's stuck,' she says. 'That's kind of the same thing.'

'No, it's not,' he says, and then splashes across the water, coat flapping behind him like wings. He drops the toolbox on the sand beside him.

'The water. Never deep here. So. Nothing to worry about.'

He's so out of breath Helena worries he might keel over right here. There's something watchful about the hunch in his shoulders. He frowns and pulls his beard back against the gusts.

'Uh,' he says. 'Not to be personal. But, well. You weren't trying to – well, you know—'

'Trying to what?'

'You know. Go in there.'

'What? Oh! No! Fuck, no. No. I was just. I don't know. Stopped for a look.'

'Oh. OK. Good. Phew.'

He blows out a big sigh, a great release of tension in his shoulders.

'People come down here to do that,' he says. 'All the time. It's fucking awful.'

'Yeah, no. No way. Not me.'

She leans sideways from the roof to lift the umbrella over him.

'I can give you a ride,' she says. 'Back up to your house. It's totally fine. To apologise.'

'Kind of you. I have spare towels, too.'

'Cool.' Now she leans the other way, winkles her keys from her pocket, presses the button that makes the boot pop open.

'In you hop,' she says, and then bumslides, jeans squeaking, down the windscreen to the bonnet and onto the sand, getting the toolbox before he can lift it and carrying it to the car-boot.

*

The car whines against the steep climb up along the road the old man shows her.

They pass through a copse of fruit-trees. Moss coats their bark. Mangoes and pineapples lie in a bright, rotted mash hovered over by wasps. Fruit pops under her wheels. The smell all around is sour with fermentation. Fat ants run in trains from the gobs of fruit.

'I'm Myles, by the way.'

'Helena. You lived in Mexico long?'

He flaps a hand.

'Oh, forever. '73, something like that. I'm from Kentucky. After that, Queens in New York. And then it got really weird in the U.S., if you were "active politically".'

He does the bunny-ears quotes with his fingers.

'So you ran away to Mexico,' she says.

'Classic move,' Myles says.

'I'd love to know where you run to if you're already from Mexico,' she says, her voice tight. In the holding cell she'd kept her eyes on the floor because of the cameras. One woman – stippled with blood where her hair had been pulled out – said their faces were cross-referenced from crowd photos taken by drones.

'It used to be easy to get off the grid here,' says Myles.

'The grid *is* the map here,' Helena says. She has a friend who won't even use rideshare apps. It's why she hasn't even turned her phone on since she left the city, hasn't let anybody know she's out, alive and safe, more or less.

The road leads through an open gate into a yard fringed by wind-stooped trees. From here, even through the rain-fog, she can see all the way down to the tracks she left across the beach. She pulls up and parks beside a shipping container. It has a chimney attached to its side that's puffing grey smoke into the dark. The light glowing in the windows is the mellow orange of a sectioned fruit.

'You don't have a car?' she says.

'Ah. Stolen,' Myles says.

'Shit.'

'Yeah. It's. Well. What can I tell you.'

Inside, a fire is burning down slowly in the grate, the ocote wood popping, releasing a smell as thick and sleepy as incense. She sees a large A3 photo of two black kids stood up in a canoe, a boy and a girl maybe aged nine and eleven. He's leaning on a small fishing-rod, her on the oar. The filter over the image is purple-grey, so their skin and their eyes and the water of the river all look like one kind of smoke.

'From the Costa Chica,' Myles says. 'Cuajinicuilapa.'

He lifts a smaller portrait. 'The kids' mother.' She's standing in the doorway of a whitewashed house, holding a scraper to the jawbone of an ass.

'I was in film production for a while. Here. But it's a weird world to be in if you're black or whatever. So I got out. Did photography instead. Just of my people. Black people.'

He slides the photo of the mother behind the children, then shuffles out another. A girl of about seven is holding up a mask as tall as her body. It's got large metal horns like a bison's, hung with black tassels of horsehair, its face part-boar, part-man, an underbite of tusks curving up, a blond goatee hanging down almost to her knees. Noticing the mask's teeth – white and flat, like a horse's – it puts a jump of fright through her chest.

'I don't think you can know how to light our skin right if you're not in our skin, you know? Amount of adjustment I have to do. Even fucking cameras are racist, man.' He chuckles a little, but sadly, then taps the rim of the photo he's holding.

'This kid here, she got deported to Honduras. Not long after. Her and her mother. Police didn't believe they'd been born here.'

Helena looks around the room, her gaze catching on a framed cloth flag: three horizontal lines, black, then white, then tan.

'Garifuna flag,' says Myles. 'They kicked the British out of San Vicente.'

'So it's all African art?' Helena says. 'The stuff you collect?'

Myles wags a finger.

'No, sir. All Mexican and Central American.' He points at a shelf. 'That statuette, with the kerchief, it's from Coahuila. The Mascogos, they're called, Black Seminoles and Muskegee who set up there back before the Civil War in the U.S. It's cool up there, man, sand looks like lilac at sunset. Big neon-striped cactus. And if you're at a wedding or a funeral there you'll hear those Gospel-singer handclaps. Surreal how it all stays alive.'

He clicks his tongue, makes a crease of his mouth, shaking his head.

'Hidden Mexico, man. Too hidden. But you can taste it, though, the similarities. The peanut sauce round here, all the kale, the collard greens that turn up in the soups and stews, yeah, for sure, and in some places they got these triangular corn-cakes, same as in the South.'

He pauses and smiles.

'One day, too, right, down at the market? Ordered some of that chicharrón in salsa verde, and boom, this, like, rush, man, you know? Pure, clear picture of my father standing at the skillet, Sunday afternoon, frying up cracklings, trying to get home from Queens via his tastebuds.'

He shakes his head.

'Turns out this place is, like, central to the African-Mexico thing. They say this guy right here, they say he came here to die.'

Myles reaches up, taps a framed image on the wall. It's a rust-splotched lithograph showing a tall, thoughtful man, serene in linens, holding a rifle.

'Basically the Mexican Toussaint,' Myles says. 'Picked his successor, high-tailing it out of his kingdom, wanting to prevent a King Lear scenario.'

He shrugs.

'I rocked up in Mexico City. For some Altman movie. Asked some folks where I might go to cool the heels. They say to go to this town. The first thing I see off the bus is a man playing the accordion, and I blink and see the blind guy who did the same outside the church back in Kentucky. I was here and not here.'

'Off the grid,' Helena says.

'In my head.' Myles nods. 'Mothers queuing up to get their daughters' diplomas framed. All these pictures of home, the tamales, the crate of beer at the foot of the old folks' cane-chairs on those do-nothing afternoons. Enough to make me change my flight.'

Helena doesn't say anything for a moment. She feels an elation lifting under her ribs, maybe it's urgency, possibility. She thought the police had stamped it out of her, but there it is, thrumming away, like a bird under her shirt.

*

The tunnel feeling of the forests on the edges of Chiapas, after secondary school, when her time was her own; awake earlier than her friends, sneaking off to a nature reserve, through the sleeping town, Zapatista flags hanging from the balconies. All the birds dozing and even the streetlights off. The only light in a doorway, an old man knelt before a bowl of amber wax over a fire. She watched him trail string through the metal bowl, hanging each loaded wick on a hoop of wood, turning and turning until the wax fattened at one end.

*

In the bathroom, Helena pulls off her trainers. The blood on the soles of her feet has dried her socks to her skin. The shower-water stings with the many bruises and scratches on her shoulders and back.

It was a march in honour of murdered women. She and Andrew, an Irish guy from college. All the signs, *vergas violadoras a la licuadora*, *get behind us or get out of our way* – everywhere they'd gone, they'd trailed shards of pavements behind them, leaving the statues that lined Reforma tattooed with spray-paint, some tumbled, a few heads cut off.

This country had been trying to kill her since she was, what, eleven, twelve? In school they'd recited the names of all the rivers, TV news had shown women's, girls' bodies coming out of Río Balsas, Río Lerma, Río de los Remedios, their faces greenish and swollen, maybe with the 'Z' of a cut along her dress, etching her skin. But, running with the others, yelling, the finger at the cops, that weight lifted from her again. Until, putting flowers in a vent in the metal wall in front of the Palacio Nacional, tear-gas struck her in the face, dropping right when the riot cops had charged. Blind, coughing, unable to stand, she was hauled into a van crammed to the doors with others, away to the precinct and the incessant perma-daylight of the electric lights. So many of them the police hadn't even pressed charges, and so, shaky, blinking, she'd staggered all the way home.

A new security guard watched her as she went through the lobby of her apartment, beside him a trolley of dwarf palms, ferns and monsteras. He watched the blood drip from her foot, said nothing, and then started texting on his phone.

She'd packed fast then, stuffing as little as she needed into her bag, checking the windows every couple of seconds, looking out for a squad-car to pull up. But nobody had come, and she'd ran all the way down to the underground car park and started driving. The eucalyptus trees under the streetlights had the slim bodies of dancers. Through the window of a shut Oxxo someone had chucked a bike so hard that the axles had forked. Under the dark sky, the buildings seemed a yellow tooth in an enormous skull, the whole city a single, hungering thing that would never let her out.

The adrenaline has washed out of her body now, leaving only a hungover sort of feeling. She considers taking the sharp corners of the toothpaste tubes and drawing red exclamation marks from her wrists to the soft of her elbow.

She towels herself. Her phone lies in her jeans. She leaves it where it is and finishes drying and dressing.

She emerges from the bathroom, Myles is kneeling on the couch looking with a frown through the window. A tomato, a chile, an onion, and some eggs are lying abandoned on a chopping-board by the sink.

'All OK?'

The pigs from the motorway have come all the way in, nosing around the yard, nosing at the sandbags propped by Myles' door, the last of the sun gleaming on their backs.

She was seeing an artist, Diego, for a while. She knew him from recovery meetings. These pigs reminded her of him, the same two-speed switch – either anxiety or indifference all the time.

'They're cute.'

'You the one's going to be hosing my yard off, then?' Myles says. 'I get nervous at anything unexpected in the yard. It's getting so strange around here.'

'Same as everywhere.'

Myles takes his glasses off and knuckles his eyes.

'Narcos. Zetas. Kids – I don't know, they do terrible things. They threw a body out of the pickup. Right into my yard. He looked like something you'd see in the market. Just this flayed lump, red with blood, black with dirt.'

'Jesus.'

'I took him to the hospital. He wasn't alive. But I wasn't going to the police.'

He sounds exhausted.

'They took my car there, at the hospital. I came back out. It was gone. Just two days ago. I've been paralysed.'

Walking out of the gym one night, one man had pushed Helena to the ground, another pulled her to her knees and clamped a hand over her mouth and put a gun to the back of her head. The barrel was cold and bumped off the small nub of bone there, leaving a scar she can still feel. A car's headlights caught their three shapes and began to honk. The gun clicked and for a second she thought she was dead, but the men ran off, howling. The car kept going. The crickets kept pulsing. The music from the club further up the road kept thudding. A couple walked past, laughing. What almost happened to her had happened by itself, like weather.

Myles is still looking out the window, squinting a little. He's a silly man, and an American; he doesn't get that Mexico is not a place to escape to, but that doesn't mean she wants him hurt.

'I can help get you out,' she's about to say, but then lights come bumping up the road. The pigs shuffle upright in the driveway. One of them's the sow from earlier, the bruise of the bumper on her flank. There's the smooth roar of a big engine, and, above that, tubas and trumpets, a brash norteño tenor. The headlights whiten Myles' yard. The music is as loud as the engine. A huge yellow Dodge RAM appears, a Santa Muerte decal on the bonnet, a man's arm hanging through the window, a large pistol in its hand. It stops with a breaking-bone click of the brakes, cants forward on its wheels, jiggles back, settles. The door opens. A couple of nearby pigs waddle towards the man's hand but he whacks at their snouts and they squeal and cower back into the rest of the throng.

'Oh, Jesus,' Myles says.

Other pigs cluster forwards, bumping the door, nuzzling, sniffing, jockeying the man. He pushes the door against them and lashes out with a boot, but more pigs surge forward. He lashes out again with the gun, then aims it, but one pig snatches a bite at his wrist, and he yowls, dropping the gun in the mud.

'Fuck's sake,' comes someone's voice from inside the jeep, the man is yanked from view, the door shuts, and it reverses out of the driveway and into the road, pursued by the whole herd of pigs who follow them into the dark.

The rain-fog swirls in the security lights and away, beyond the rucked-up mud and pigshit, the ivory-handled pistol glints in the driveway.

'I'm never eating one of those ever again,' Myles says.

He sinks onto the couch with a noise like a deflating bouncy castle.

They'll come back for the gun, beat down his door, start beating him and worse, which is why Helena says, 'It's fine, don't worry,' and reaches for the plastic envelope and begins slotting the photos in, the woman holding the ass's jawbone, the two kids in the canoe, and last of all, that mask whose dance would turn the impure to stone.

'What should I pack next? Anything you can leave behind?'

Myles laughs.

'Apart from the photos? Just about all of it.'

*

At the bottom of the slope back to the beach, the sand is glazed white with drying salt, which flies up behind them in fantails that look like light through water. Of the pigs, there's no sign except mucky hoofmarks that fade towards a dirt road.

Helena flips the indicator and takes them onto the highway. Over in the distance, where the sky is still dark, a weathervane is turning against pulsating reefs of lilac cloud. The air buffeting through the window tastes cool and wet.

'Not to boast,' Myles says, 'But, well, me and the gang, back in the day, we had COINTELPRO to deal with, you know.'

He spreads his hands.

'And I managed OK.'

'Yeah, OK,' Helena says. 'I'm going to need to hear all of this.'

Myles laughs gently, pinkish light from the rising sun playing over his glasses.

'Find yourself a small town,' he says, 'and take it from there.'

There was that moment near Chiapas when she was alone: sky and lake tinged a deep pink by the early light. She slides a cigarette from the packet, offers one to Myles, lights up, feels the nicotine quicken the uplift into an ebullition she almost wants to call hope. The smoke hovers like parting curtains. She watches it hover there. Outside, the sow with the bruised flank nuzzles her snout against a head of corn, its kernels still intact.

DIVE

Halfway up the slope to the settling tank, Maya looks around. This is where she is meant to meet the trash-diver for an interview. She sees a van with the turquoise SACMEX logo and its toothy Pre-Columbian insignia, and wonders what god it's meant to be: Tláloc? From the van a team of men are lifting equipment – a long, kinked umbilicus of metal and plastic; a radio console that's so big and red that it could be a chunk of fire-engine.

She'd prefer to be out in Tepito, talking to the uncle of that girl who vanished in Puebla. The last she'd been seen was at a party with an up-and-coming senator. She knows the uncle: he used to be a source, and now he's a friend – a fruit shop owner called Osito, old-school, working-class, gay, sometimes maybe sells guns on the side, always keeps an eye out for her when she's poking around his neighbourhood. It's not just that she wants to write the story: she wants the story to help him. But Daniel, her editor, hauled her into the office, forced her into this stupid daily story about a trash-diver or something.

'Sewer divers,' he said, beaming. 'What do you think?'

'I think I've read the "sewer divers" story every year, for, like, six years now.'

For years, the city government has had only one trash-diver on its books, even when the blocked drains cause the kind of floods that bring typhoid and cholera.

'Yes, yes, but they've hired a new one.'

He gave her a cheesy pair of finger-guns and an even cheesier crease-mouth smile, a side parting in his silver hair like some kind of late-stage version of Jarvis Cocker.

'Is that it?' Maya said. 'There's a new trash diver, and *that*'s the story?'

'Yes,' he said, still doing the face.

Daniel lowered his feet from the desk and slid his chair towards his laptop. His fingers clicked on the keys. 'Let me just email you all the details. They've had this assistant going for years beside the main guy, and he's got a big solo dive, so, tomorrow, bright and early – or, well, *dark* and early – you'll watch the new guy. Well: new*ish* guy. And you'll get me a lovely twelve hundred words for our environmental' – he waggled his fingers in the air – '"thingy".'

'Series.'

'Yes, our environmental series thingy. Now, go have a lovely day.'

Typing with one hand, he waved with the other without looking up from the screen.

Maya turned her head, felt the meat of her neck give a weird grunt. She'd been waking up sprawled all over the place, unused to the bed with just one person in it. Her ex is in Guanajuato now, living with *his* ex, because they patched it all up, didn't they, over a timeline that's tangled up in a way that Maya prefers not to speculate about. All he left was a blank space on the wall where his flatscreen had been. It's strange, but she can't stop eating her breakfast in front of it. He's also a journalist, kind of – a food critic, that is, his belle-lettristic tweets have an audience of fifty thousand.

Maya took a second to get up from the chair, then stood in front of his desk for a second.

'Daniel,' she said, 'this story is crap. I hate it.'

Daniel didn't even stop typing. He frowned like a pained therapist, then said, 'Aw, tell me more.'

'I wanted to go out to Tepito today,' she said. 'Find out about that girl. The one who went missing from that deputy's party. I know her uncle – I go to his fruit shop sometimes.'

'Well, if you're friends,' Daniel said, 'you can go see him whenever, can't you?'

Maya didn't say anything. She didn't leave the office, either.

Daniel stopped typing, all of the jokiness gone.

'You know what they say,' he said, resting his chin on his interlaced fingers, 'about earning credit from your editors with daily churn and burn stories so you can do the investigative stuff?'

Maya shut her eyes for a second and said, 'Yes.'

'And you know how I don't have one single such churn and burn byline from you in, oh, perhaps' – he squinted theatrically at the screen, clicking around – '*seven* months, while my inbox fills with your "updates" and your "one last thing" and your "one more week".'

He clicks hard on the mouse, his hand rising with an arced flourish, then says, 'I think somebody may need to remind me that she is a reporter, before I can feel as though allowing her to do the detective thing is the best use of our increasingly stretched time and increasingly fucked budget. No?'

'Yeah, alright,' Maya said, and went to leave the office.

'Glad we agree,' Daniel said, his voice bright again. 'Now, dark and early, at the reservoir, and then maybe it'll be back to our detective games.'

'Yes, lieutenant,' Maya said, and let the door click shut behind her.

*

She climbs the slope towards the tank that's about to be unblocked. When one of the crew members sees her, he waves and comes walking down the path towards her. He's tall, even his face is heavily tattooed. His baggy vest and shaven head give him the vibe of a cholo, with the V-shaped torso of people who work out seriously, though there's no threat in his smile.

'Interviewer, right?' he says, his hand out to shake hers. Little skulls and knives and tarot-looking people cluster on his forehead, his eyebrows, his cheeks. Chicano cursive and Tupac blackletter mottos on his arms and chest. 'Maya, is it?'

'Yeah, that's me.' He's weirdly friendly for an assistant. 'You with the diver?'

He laughs and says, 'I am the diver. My name's Adonai.'

'Oh.' She hadn't looked at the details Daniel sent.

The guy waves at the air like she's apologised. 'Nah, it's cool. You need a coffee or something? We got some in the van. And there's time before the dive. You can do the questions and everything like that if you want.'

'Sure.' She always tries to sound like she's indulging the men she interviews, because it pisses them off, but it feels wrong with him.

'Cool,' he says. 'Let me just get changed real quick.'

A heavy-set man with curly hair sets up the equipment. He connects a plug and the white glare of a floodlight illuminates the field of trash floating on the surface of the cistern. The odour in the air reminds her of reading Dante at university, the rain of shit and the marsh of even more shit.

Adonai opens the door of a Portakabin by the water. He's pulled on a neoprene suit and he's holding a coffee cup out to her.

'Come on in,' he says. 'I've never been interviewed before. Hope I'm doing this right.'

'If you could just hold that,' Maya says, levelling the camera at him. He's under the light but a stray dog is pissing on the wall behind him so she has to wait for it to stop before she takes a photo. Then she aims again, only for a cardboard box to hop past in the breeze.

'Fuck,' she says, and he laughs. The smile is what she needs: it will take the edge off the tattoos. 'Cool. Thanks.'

'That was easy,' he says.

Maya follows him up the three steps into the prefab. There's none of the locker-room fug she'd been expecting. There's more space and light, a huge map on the wall with the city's pipelines highlighted red and blue like a medical textbook showing veins.

Adonai pulls a chair out from behind a desk and sits down on it, gesturing to the one next to it. His diving-mask lies dismantled on the desk. He starts scrubbing inside the screw-holes with a nail-varnish applicator brush. 'I'm a bit behind today – bit of glue hit my mask last time I was down. It's a fucker to clean off.'

'Do what you have to do.' Maya sits down, puts her recorder on the table and gets her notebook out. 'Pretty bad down there. You ever wonder why you do it?'

Adonai frowns. He tries to smile, then huffs a laugh out through his nose. She feels bad. Throwing them with the first question is the right thing to do to politicians and union bosses, but for someone like him it's maybe cruel.

'Yeah,' he says. 'Like, I get you, yeah. Like. I don't know. I go to the supermarket, yeah? And there's these individual ketchup sachets, wrapped in another plastic bag, tape around them, and I'm like, yo, OK, so whoever made this shit was like "We have a planet to kill, there's no time for fucking around". But for me it's not the bad water gets to me. It's the trees.'

He puts down the nail-varnish brush and begins screwing the mask back together. The tinkle of the screws as he chases them with his big fingers sounds like the start of rain.

'Like, the ones we have here — you ever notice how many eucalyptus there are in the city? Literally the worst tree.' His fingers work the screws in. Around the knuckles she sees a blurry crown of thorns.

'Thirsty motherfucker. The roots break up the pavements, split the pipes, and so that's even more water. And on top of *that*, right, once they're mature? They start secreting this oil under their bark that turns flammable.'

She looks at her notepad for the next question, but there's no stopping his flow of talk.

'Just these giant thirsty lighters standing around waiting to blow,' he says. 'Oh, and the smoke is toxic, too. Obviously.'

'So what made you go into this?' Maya asks. 'If it's all so hopeless.'

He huffs out a breath. 'Guilt, you know. Just me and my ex had this restaurant. Nothing fancy. Breakfast place. But it just got to me after a while.'

He lifts the mask above his head, checking the parts are flush.

'Kept seeing the drains as these throats that couldn't swallow. Or you offer people a plastic thing to take home, or you use the cardboard ones with a laminate on top, with these fibres that work their way into the fish, into people's babies, whatever.' He shrugs. 'So, whatever you do, I guess, is the answer, whatever you do, if you're not doing something to make it better, you're making it worse.'

'But everyone's making it worse, no matter what.' Maya eases back in her seat, crossing one leg over the other.

'Right. Yeah.' He blows into the mask and condensation blooms across the glass. 'This city needs way more money on cleaning out trash, everyone knows that. I won't even get chewed out for saying it.'

He lifts a rubber snood from the corner of the table and pulls it over his head. 'But, whatever, I'm down in it, and that makes me sleep easier. Can put my hands up and be like, "I was swimming round in goop and plastic fibres for fifteen hours today, don't blame me for shit".'

The rubber of the snood whaps against his neck.

'That to keep the smell out?' Maya says.

'In theory.' He blows into the mask one last time then slings it around his neck.

'So. A restaurateur turned diver.' She taps her notebook with her pen. 'Bit of a shift, skill-set wise.'

'Oh, really I'm just going back. The water was my first love, you know? See, I'm from Ensenada.'

'You don't sound it,' Maya cuts in.

He laughs, but not like it's funny. 'LA, DF, Juárez, people have strong ways of talking. So you imitate them, or whatever. Otherwise they make fun of you.' He blows into a glove. 'This thing, yeah? It's, like, stab-proof. Syringes and shit. Coat hangers. Current catches them, flings it at you, it's like a javelin.'

'A coat hanger?'

He shrugs. 'Someone had a blockage, they go after the lump, and flush sucks it down, I'm guessing.'

'What's the worst thing you found?' Maya asks.

He scratches under his chin and says, 'Probably the fridge. Must have been a sinkhole took it down. The street was disgusting, drains boiling up, like fucking lava, just black mud and slurry, prawn-shells, bits of tortillas. Parts of people, too. Jeffrey Dahmer shit, you know? But mostly, I don't know, stuff coming at me, at speed, battering the mask, some of it maybe sharp enough to tear the suit, break the glass, and I'm thinking, "Oh, shit, could this be it?", but it never has been, so far.'

He velcros shut his boots.

'But mostly I like it down there. The tides down here, they're like a big heart I'm inside the veins of. And mostly stuff bumps at, like, zero miles per hour. '

'LA, DF, Juárez,' she reads. 'Tough places to be if you like being near the sea, I'd think. Big cities.'

'Well, LA's on the coast, so.' He rubs his hand over the back of his skull. 'I don't know, I got into some stuff that I'm not into now, and. Now I'm not into it.'

'I see.' She has him now. She taps the space under her left eye, where he's tattooed with crosses and teardrops and says nothing.

'Yep.'

He holds her gaze, but his eyes are flat and tell her nothing. He gets to his feet, saying, 'So, I should probably get ready.' He's walking out the door, and she's following him. 'You'll come watch, I assume?'

He takes off the glove to shake her hand, and off he goes, out the door, down the steps towards the crane that's pulled up beside the cistern wall. Maya watches him climb onto the rusted metal cage at the end of the crane's arm.

'Bring me up something juicy,' she says. 'Nothing less than a cadaver.'

Adonai looks at her, a twitch of a frown across his eyebrows, but then he turns to the guy manning the crane and says, 'Any questions she has, Julián, will you take care of them?'

'Sure thing,' he says, then gives Maya a shy wave as she nears the crane. A red console blurts static beside her, then the crane hums and raises the diver high over concrete walls climbed black with muck. Above the cistern, the metal inlet grid is piled up with rags. Tyres float there, rusted wires showing through the rubber, the rest of the scrim too rotted and softened for her to tell what any of it was. Even through the blue dental mask, the smell of the cistern is a gust of everything awful – eggs and brine, the sticky vegetable-rot smell, something sour and milky too awful to be milk.

The crane is over the water now. In his red suit and orange helmet, he's like an astronaut. He's holding a long, rusted piece of rebar, and, against the sophistication of the rest of his gear, it looks almost comical, like an ancient harpoon. The arm of the crane extends outwards, then lowers him towards the trash. Over the shoulder of the guy is the view from the GoPro on Adonai's helmet. It looks like he's descending onto the surface of a planet, though it disaggregates into plastic bottles, coffee-cups, cellophane wrappers, soaked cardboard, a rat turning around and around beside a blackened orange and a tuna sandwich. The diver's feet hit it and the goop climbs his body. Water shunts against his goggles, a green-black filter over everything on the screen. The diver gives a thumbs-up, raises his rebar, and then he's gone. Maya's breath catches.

Half-eaten by static, she hears his voice. 'Getting out of the basket now,' he says, 'water's very heavy – crawling now. Blockage three metres down.'

She hears gravel tink against the glass of his visor, the echo massive.

'Past two metres now. Going to feel for the blockage.'

'How's he going to know?' Maya says to the man at the console.

'Here's what he's doing,' the man says, putting out his arms and standing with his legs further apart, in an 'X'. 'He's just floating in this starfish shape. So he can feel where the blockage is by the way the water is moving funny.' He laughs. 'You can't train that kind of thing.'

For what feels like a long time, there's just the sound of his breath and things bumping against him. When he finally speaks – 'Yeah, OK, there it is, veering down and left' – the staticky blurt makes Maya jump. At the console, Julián sits forward, the knuckles of one hand against his mouth.

'Going to engage now I think,' he says, then the static smoothes out as he dives, and the next clear sound that Maya hears is the tinking of a hammer.

'What do you think you've got down there?' Julián says into his microphone.

'Ah, that's a surprise, man,' the diver says back.

'You fucker,' Julián says, 'We're not going to send a winch down, then, I take it.'

'No, no, I've got it.' The diver grunts. There's a tearing. 'Yep, nearly done.'

In the chair, at the console, Julián gives a little punch of the air.

'Animal, vegetable, or mineral?' Julián says into the mic.

'Mixture,' Adonai says. 'Returning to the basket now.'

Whatever it is that he's holding, she can hear the feathery drag of it troubling the water around his head and shoulders. Bubbles swirl as he lifts his leg over the bars into the basket.

'OK, I'm in,' he says.

Julián waves to the driver in the truck, who flashes his lights and begins to raise the arm of the crane – the wetted layer of trash parts, white branches slowly growing upwards. Bottles and cans stick to the twigs, wrapped in tricolour papel picado bunting from someone's *Día de*

Independencia. Then the slender trunk flows into view, and now finally there's the diver, one hand around the trunk, the other around his rebar harpoon. It's impossible to tell what kind of tree it was because the whole thing has been bleached pure white. He could be an Arctic hunter posing with a whale's skeleton.

'Yeah, pretty weird,' Julián says at the console.

The basket lowers to the bank of the cistern. Light winks on the chrome around Adonai's visor. The mesh lifts, water roars out, and the caught rags surge into the trash. The smell hits Maya like a rugby tackle. The crease of a smile appears either side of the diver's eyes as he climbs out and sits down on the grass. Julián carries a full bucket over to him, lifts it, and douses him with the contents, which fizz, bubble, and smoke. Adonai lifts off his helmet and snood while Julián fetches a second bucket to pour over his head. He giggles with the cold of it.

Maya laughs. The sound makes the diver look up. His laugh stops, his smile vanishes, and he says, 'You get what you needed?'

'What, no cadaver?' she says.

'You ever see one of those down there,' he says, peeling off his gloves, 'you wouldn't make that joke.' She can see how he was probably scary back in the day. She wonders how his girlfriend became his ex. The second glove snaps against his palm.

'If you can't joke about it,' Maya says, and zips up her camera-bag, 'it'll get to you in the end.' She pockets her notebook and starts walking back towards the car. Her strides are quickened by the downhill slope. She hears Julián say, 'Have a good one!' behind her, but she doesn't bother to turn or raise her hand in a wave.

*

Maya sits at her office-desk, glaring at the foot-long she picked up for lunch. It's dank with bad sauce and dropping scribbles of onion, the kind of thing she'd have sent a photo of to her ex, the kind of thing he'd reply, *Baby, you only get one lunch a day! Use it wisely!* She reaches in her bag for the voice-recorder. The sooner she makes herself listen to her own voice, the sooner she can get to Osito at the fruit-shop. Her phone clanks against her make-up mirror, which shifts against her pepper spray, then her panic button knocks against her knuckles, but there's no tape recorder. Her breath goes in hard.

Daniel moves through the office, sifting through a basket of post. They get a couple of rounds a day. Often they're tips. Sometimes they're threats. As he nears Maya's desk, she sees he's carrying a small parcel for her.

'This one feels... bulgy,' he says, shaking it. 'A... *bomb*?'

She slits open the envelope and there's the recorder, the power still on, the battery fine, the WAV file about forty minutes longer after she'd left it there on the desk in the Portakabin.

'It's a sign from God,' Daniel says, still standing by her desk, flicking through the post.

'Of?'

'Of, you should get that transcript done.' He swans towards his office. 'Or it's your badge and gun, detective.'

Maya plugs her headphones in and loads up the transcription software. The recording looks way longer than their interview: on the visualisation of the file, there's a gap after it, and then the spikes and troughs and soft wave-lines of someone talking. She jumps the cursor to where the line picks up again. It's a man's voice, older, tired.

'It's Julián. The guy on the crane. I wouldn't usually do this but you were tough on our boy out there today.' She hears him clear his throat, hears a chair being pulled out, and then the buzzy rasp of someone talking way too close to the speaker. 'Adonai can be a grumpy little bastard, but he's a saint in his own grumpy little way. Yeah, he was into some stuff, that stuff you wanted to hear about, the gangs, the drugs, fights, things that could have gotten him killed.'

He clears his throat slowly, hitchingly, and Maya lifts the recorder away from her ear. 'Our boy, he misses the sea. The only place you get an oceanic feeling far from the ocean is from the lulling pulse of something else in your body, from the big warm drown of too many drinks that are never enough – a tidal motion in the blood.'

Maya reaches out for the laptop, types *Cleaning up the city after cleaning up his life?*, but then there's another dragging noise of throat-clearing from Julián.

'He is my son, in a way – I brought him into our fellowship and our meetings, and because I brought him into this job. And because, before this boy dived, he flew. He was meant to be a dancer, you understand. His parents told him to be a lifeguard, get his Plan B lined up first. Except not even Plan B was possible, because our boy splits his Achilles tendon in half.'

The man's knuckles rap the table. 'It's not my place to take his inventory. But the split's still there.' He clears his throat, blows out a breath.

'You know, after humans are gone, all our last traces are going to be, like, twenty-six inches of glittery stuff at the bottom of the sea. All of human history, every century, every war, every landfill, just a little glitter, then a scatter, then gone.'

The man laughs, then clears his throat, then laughs again. 'And, yes, OK, I can hear you ask, "How'd he get into ballet to begin with?" Last thing you'd think a norteño boy's going to be into. But you'll have to ask him. I'll drop this recorder over to him, have him return it. Maybe he will leave you his number and you can ask him yourself.'

There's a rustle and a fumble, then a beep, and then the recording stops dead. The red light blinks. Maya sits back against the chair, working her palm into the curve of pain in her shoulder. She turns the recorder over. There's a scrap of a Post-It, the name *Adonai*, and a number. She types it into her phone, deletes it, types it in, deletes it, and then finally takes a breath and adds him. She can't think of a message. But at least she has her subhead. She deletes *Cleaning Up the City*, and then adds the title she'll put above the new draft, the one she wants to get to Daniel before evening, so she can stop into the fruit shop in Tepito to find out more about Osito's niece. *Like Dancing Underwater*, she writes, and then she starts typing.

*

It's Saturday afternoon, and Maya's at Parque Delta, the mall-din like a swimming-pool around her. She's got ages to kill, and every shop is a scrum. Osito was more angry than cut up about the lost niece, and wouldn't tell her anything more than he 'had a plan' and 'not to worry.' Which did worry her, but not enough to push Adonai out of her mind.

She lets a string of four-year-olds pelt yelping past her, a woman following behind. Until it's time for them to meet, she drifts from floor to floor, slowly circling towards the little coffee island that Adonai suggested. A girl sprints past, a wild laugh skirling up out of her, long pigtails bobbing. Maya's eyes alight on a pair of gold trainers. They're on offer too. Onitsukas, real ones, but she sees the size of the queue for the tills and sees there's just two minutes until Adonai's due to arrive. So, looking over her shoulder, she stoops to slide the trainers under a bunch of trousers, out of sight of other shoppers, though as she's getting up, she catches sight of Adonai sitting at one of the coffee-island's tables. He gives her an embarrassed wave.

She looks up and over at the queue and a woman waiting for the boy at the till. He's forcing bubble-wrap into the box around a pair of shoes. The bubble-wrap looks like octopus-suckers. She looks back at Adonai, waves her hand, because why keep someone waiting over a pair of shoes, and moves through everyone, out of the door towards him.

CHEFS

His hair rumpled, his face seamed with pillow-scars, Diego wakes in his hotel-room, awaiting a donut he ordered in his dream. Then he remembers where he is, groans, and reaches for the carafe of water the cleaning service left out with the mints the same clean white as the room.

High-heeled footsteps clop towards and then past his door. It's Magda, the director of the poetry course he's teaching, here in this town an hour south of the city, a pretty tourist town famous for its cave spas and hot springs, even back in pre-Hispanic times.

'I hope he doesn't sleep through this thing,' he hears Magda say. 'Why's he not there?'

'There is *a lot* of alcohol there, Magda,' says her assistant.

'He's got two years,' Magda replies blithely. She's wrong. It's six. But whatever. Either way, he has to be normal now. At the bathroom sink, he sluices the cobwebs from his mouth then goes to the balcony, taking in the view of the villa-style hotel's grounds. Glowing with fairy lights, the tunnel of wisteria leads all the way to a big-tiled square, students and faculty and waiting staff milling around. A pyramid of tulip-glasses gleams on the white-covered tables at the back. They have those big traditional jugs of mezcal, but it isn't *that* much alcohol, really; he can be around it, as long as he doesn't drink any, he thinks. He slides his feet into espadrilles. He's slept in what passes for his dress clothes.

All month, he's been fearing these students. He's only accidentally a poet. He did an album of cut-and-pastes from notebooks he'd jotted in those years he was on heroin, joined lines together with an algorithm, letting them spill around enough to seem like the fragmentation of addiction to people who had never been addicted to anything in particular. An art press put out sixty pages of it, which won a prize big enough for people to want him to teach other people how to write poems, even though he doesn't know how.

He feels his fraudulence giddily, like a heist he's about to pull off.

After all, he thinks, tidying himself at the mirror, all these students are paying for is hope, to be sent back into the concrete world full of the dream that making stuff can make everything OK.

He leaves the room with a glass of iced water from the carafe so the waiters won't offer him a wine-glass. This could be the easiest gig of his life, he thinks, walking, munching ice, towards the crowd, his eyes so lost in the veinwork of ivy and wisteria above him that he nearly chest-bounces a woman off the path and into the grass.

'Oh, shit,' he says, as she laughs and does a little antelope-totter backwards from him along the gravel path. Clear mezcal splashes from her shot-glass onto the web of her hand. 'I'm so fucking sorry.'

'No, that's fine, honestly.' She sucks at her hand. She is incredible: it hits him as a sinking of the blood. She has a loose, chiffony dress on. This is awful. He sees the little bone nubs of her shoulders under the straps. He'd like to bite them, run his face down her arm, taste the tongue-drying salt of sweat mixing with deodorant. Girls like this are the kind he could never date before. They smelled too clean next to the sourness of his addiction. Now, though, he has all sorts of ways to conceal this.

'You're brave to be out on this in heels,' he says, because she hasn't gotten out of his way.

She laughs. She has a slight hunch to her shoulders. She probably got made fun of in school for being too tall.

'Do you like the hotel?' she says.

'Ah, yeah, nice to be anywhere like this, really.' He points over his shoulder. 'I'm staying over there.'

'Oh! Near mine. Room Five. Pool view.' Her tone of voice has that blank chirpiness to it. Teaching doesn't start until Monday, so now he's got two days of knowing where she lives and wondering if he should knock on her door some evening. He can no longer tell if or when anybody is flirting with him. Politeness has made the young so boring; they'll say anything and mean anything for as long as they have to, and all because they're scared. Diego never figured out how to be charming, only apologetic, and now he's too chippy to be apologetic.

'Noisy, then, I suppose.' He clears his throat, looks towards the drinks-table. Now that he really thinks about it, he can't see any sparkling water anywhere, not even juice.

'Thankfully no kids around.' She pauses, looks down at her glass for a second, then says, 'I just wanted to say how brave your work is.' She does a little cough-laugh. 'Or are you tired of people calling your work "brave"?'

Even if this isn't flirting, he imagines it'd be easy to make it — and there'd be two ways it would go then. One: he'd flop around in her admiration of his pain like the Dying Gaul, while her own pain grew slowly out of control. Which is what happened in his first sober relationship. When it ended, she sent him photos of her naked chest, the space between her breasts pocked red-black from still-smoking cigarette-burns, the caption read, 'I am trying to burn you out of me and it will not work.' Or, two: boring her off him. *Honesty, open-mindedness and willingness: with these we are well on our way.* That's what they say at the beginnings of Narcotics Anonymous meetings. He can do the first one, he supposes.

'A little bit, yes,' Diego says to her. 'Sorry.'
'Oh.'

'That's alright,' he says, even though she didn't apologise. He leans against one of the posts holding up the wisteria, puts a hand through his hair. 'See, I try to destroy everything I write. Every couple of months. I tell myself, "This is it, done". But the words keep seeping up, don't they, a black leak from who knows what cut inside me, drip, drip, drip, filling me up until I've got to drain it out.' He scratches under his chin. She has taken another step back. 'I'd like to see what would be there if I was ever able to drain it all out entirely, and then shut up, "a rugged bed of stone the colour of rust, scarred and porous, littered with bright grit".'

He's quoting himself. He waits for that to sink in. He's not sure if it does. He keeps going. 'So we'll try to get you to that stage, I guess, won't we? So that we can all enjoy the silence.'

'I see. Well. Thanks,' she says. She's gripping the elbow of her arm holding the glass. 'And how are you feeling about the course and stuff?' A note of doubt has crept into her voice. Why can't she just excuse herself and go?

'I'm feeling good about it.' He hooks out a chunk of ice with his finger. A dribble of water goes down the side of his glass. He watches her watching this. 'I remember this one guy in my Narcotics Anonymous group.' He watches her reaction. 'A director. Talked about working on a fellowship in Colorado. Lost grip of himself entirely, wound up flaking LSD into himself, a shock-blanket around him, punching holes in the plaster to let the voices out of the room' – Diego's finger waggles in the air – '"and all," the director said, running a hand over his shaved scalp, "all because I couldn't face prepping for one simple lecture" – which wasn't even that funny a line, but it hit like a *punchline*, you know? The chuckles around the room bubbling over into full-on laughter.' He sweeps his hand in an arc, tracing the shape of the room. She steps back.

'Yeah.' He scratches his nose. 'So, you know, as long as nothing like that happens to me this weekend, we'll be alright, won't we?' His laugh sounds like a fox's bark. He gives her a matey pat on the shoulder, hears the flat smack of his palm on her skin. 'Excuse me, won't you? Better get a drink. I'll see you in class.' Then he's past her, eyes looking everywhere for a waiter holding anything that won't total his recovery.

He looks at the crowd for a minute, bodies unknotting in the warmth of the first couple of drinks, carillons of laughter rising up brightly towards the clouds of mosquitos and the puttering flames of the outdoor heaters. At things like this in the needle years he would totter about, saying, 'Right, right, right,' no matter what was said. A solution to all his social problems – until, of course it caused every other kind of problem.

A male student he's not yet spoken to – bearded, one of those undercut long flops of hair that Diego always finds vaguely fascistic – breezes past him, waving over his shoulder at him. The trays of drinks are loaded – sweating bottles of beer in ice-buckets, massed flutes of champagne, brimming shots of mezcal as clear as eyes. The terrace is starting to feel like a bad idea. He looks around for an alternative. Magda, the director, is talking to a camera-crew over by the pool. The mike boom makes Diego think of the fluffy antennae of a moth budging after food or light. He watches too long: the assistant, Gaby, catches his eye and waves at him to come over.

'Oh, fuck,' he says, but smiles, and returns her wave with a pinch of the fingers to say, 'Just a minute'.

The UNAM channel is filming interviews with everyone. There he was, thinking he had only one job – not to drink – and now fate's dumped this shit in his lap hasn't it.

So while Gaby watches Magda, Diego slips into the shadows. The wet grass tickles his ankles. Gleeful at escaping, he moves under the palapa and into the cool of the gym-room. The smell of rice-paper is a surprise but when his eyes adjust to the dimness he sees there's a small library here, faded encyclopedias and tattered paperbacks and old copies of *National Geographic*, with wingbacked pink velvet armchairs and little Tlaloc statues on lit plinths arranged around a low table the colour of a coffin. It's nice though. He likes it. He could curl up here and pretend he'd forgotten the interview, pretend he'd been busy talking to that student. It wouldn't quite be a lie.

The upstairs light is on. Motes twine above the spiral stairs. He climbs them, up to an attic where a pool-table stands under a perfect box of golden light, giving off that funeral smell of new varnish. He draws a cue from its slot and lays out the balls in a loose pyramid, shapes them tighter with a jiggle of the triangular rack against the baize.

Diego takes a swig and rolls an ice-flake along the wall of his mouth. As each ball thunks against the bank and lands with a hiss in the netted pockets, he can nearly hear his father's exclamation. He doesn't remember his father ever going to a cantina, or a pool-hall, or even drinking at home. His father was a mechanic who specialised in Scania trucks, which took him all over northern Mexico during the week, though he was always back by Friday evening to see Diego and Teresa. When Teresa was twelve and Diego was ten, on a job at a small garage in Zacatecas, something went wrong with the lift-table and the cabin of a truck fell right on top of him. Death would have come so fast that Diego believed his father wouldn't have even realised he's dead, can still imagine him returning to the workshop in their garage, playing some version of this resurrection in his head for almost thirty years.

Downstairs, the door clicks open. He stands, rigid, the cue like a spear. Maybe he's been up here long enough to steel himself for the interview, but he knows he hasn't: there's a flutter in his chest still like moths in a bell-jar. Something blocks the light downstairs: he sees the shadow of a hand flip the shadow of longish hair, hears a sniff, and his fear heats into anger. Footsteps begin to climb the spiral stairs. Diego looks down and sees the young man, two beer-bottles sweating in his grip and his hands tighten on the pool-cue.

'Hey,' says the young man, giving Diego a nod, his cigarette and casual gesture utterly undercut by his eyes, the ripple in his voice. 'Brought you a drink.' He proffers one of the beers. Threads of smoke fray up and reknit opaque across the cone of light over the baize. The smell brings back the taste of parties where he'd huff down lines as long as this pool-table.

The young man is walking towards him, shaking his head, saying, 'Man, you have so many crazy stories. I can't wait to hear them.'

Diego takes the beer with a numb hand. A ray of cold radiates from the skin of his face. He can't even feel the beer in his grip. Diego slides the cue back into its hole at the end of his table. He takes a step forward, his breath hissing like steam. The kid gives an awkward laugh and takes a step back so that he's nearly teetering on the edge of the stairs. Which makes him laugh again.

'Hey, whoa, now,' he begins to say, but then Diego is gripping a fistful of his black scoop-neck t-shirt.

'Cunt,' says Diego, and tips the beer down the kid's shirt. Beer glugs out, foaming in the kid's chest-hairs. 'Cunt,' says Diego again. 'Cunt, cunt, cunt.'

'Oh, what the fuck, man?' the kid yowls, clutching his soaked t-shirt, staring at it. Diego moves him out of the way, drops the bottle and shoves the kid to the carpeted ground behind him.

'Are you fucking crazy?'

Diego looks over his shoulder from the turn in the spiral, and says, 'Yes. Yes, I am.'

Downstairs, he runs across the floor, back into the dark. The terrace would be the first place that soaked idiot would look for him. Towards the pool, where the camera-crew are craning around, Magda and Gaby are on the path towards his room. He feels a groan begin in his chest, because the only other route he can see is to his car parked by the open gate. It's not even a decision: his legs are pumping him over the grass, the rhythm as monotonous as the glugging beer or 'Cunt, cunt, cunt'. He gets in, slams the door, and looks back up at the pool hall. He sees his father lifting him through the dim light, hears again the clack of the balls, his laughing. He will drive back there – all the way to Aguascalientes, their childhood home. He starts the car, whips it around in a crunching rooster-tail of pebbles. The kid is already running across the grass towards him, his face aghast.

'Shit, man,' he's saying. 'I'm sorry. I'm really sorry. I thought you could have just one beer.'

Diego lowers the window and puts his hand out. He raises his middle finger, turning it in the air behind him as he drives out of the gate and onto the grey track of the country road that corkscrews north to Mexico City and beyond.

*

It's after eleven and thickly dark by the time Diego gets into Zacatecas, a lacquer of muck crunching under the tyres of his car. He slows past the shuttered machine-shops and grocery-stores, his eyes moving back and forth between the windscreen and the red tangle of the map-line on his GPS, so that the sudden yellow crackle of fireworks startles him, and he's certain – momentarily – they've been let off for him. Then he sees the bunting above the streets, the golden bell-shaped LEDs on the fronts of the buildings, and he remembers it's Independence Day.

Diego eases his car along the last snarls of the route, down the second-last turn before the garage, and feels his heart flip slowly over. He doesn't know if the family will want to see him, if they still live there in fact, or even if they're still alive. He's looked at this sign on Street View countless times. It should be more monumental, he thinks, as he pulls in between a white Honda jeep and a little orange Suzuki Swift.

He gets out, and hears laughter and a Los Ángeles Azules song filtering down from the lit upstairs window above the garage. Just remembering all those claustrophobic family gatherings gives him a heavy, glassy feeling. Tiny shadows screech across the glass. He has no idea how to be around kids: they make him snippy and abrupt, like a cop, while crouching down to their height makes him feel even more like a cop. If I have to deal with kids during this thing I am finished, he says to himself, walking towards the door and pressing the buzzer. The walls and windows are so thin he hears the thunder of feet and adult voices now, before the window scrapes up.

'Can I help you?' says a man's voice.

Diego steps back from the shutters into his line of sight, then waves. Words are a curdled mass in his throat. He's imagined dozens of versions of this moment during the drive here, but now he can't call up a single one. The guy at the window doesn't look like who he'd imagined either – he's hefty, in need of a shave, the little spikes of his thinning hair crisp as the skin of a toffee-apple, and he doesn't look friendly. He'd imagined someone humble and soft-spoken, who'd remember everything in an instant.

Diego sucks in a breath.

'If you're selling something, we don't want it,' the guy says. 'It's a family night, you know?'

'I realise that,' Diego says. 'That's sort of why I drove up.' He nods at the shutter. 'My father worked here.'

The guy's brow gets lines and an edge comes into his voice, 'And we owe him money or what?'

'Well, no, nobody owes him anything, really,' Diego says. 'He's dead.'

'Oh.' Diego sees his fingers tap against the rim of the beer-can he's holding, then the guy says, 'Sorry for your loss', as he might have said, 'So what?'

'He worked for Scania,' Diego says. 'It was a one-off.'

The guy at the window takes a deep breath in and out, then he nods.

'Right,' he says. 'OK. I think I remember something like this.'

Diego nods. The guy must be what, five, six years older than him – old enough to have maybe been working alongside his father or uncle or whatever back in the day when the truck fell on him.

'Who is it, love?' says a woman's voice from inside.

'I'll be back in a minute, alright?' the guy says. He looks down at Diego. He taps the can, then rubs the heel of his hand against his cheek, before at last he says, 'Let me go in and talk to my father for a second.'

'Yeah, sure,' Diego says, but the window slams down before he can get to the end of the sentence. It's just him and the buzzing of the streetlight and the mucky dark of the street. All the other ways he could have done this are churning around and around, though all of them are also crap. He opens the app with the NA meeting schedules and tries to see one he can find straight after this. What is it he wants to see here, anyway – a dim room walled in posters of girls in bikinis and old football teams, a smell of oil, a liftgate that may or may not have been replaced since the early '90s?

From inside he hears the man talking, the woman's reticence. Diego already knows how it's going to be, when the window goes back up and the guy says, 'Sorry about this, but it's a family occasion. You know? A special night. So if you could just—'

'Right,' says Diego. 'Right. Yeah. No problem. I get it. And sorry. You know?'

'Sure.' The window goes down a second time. The footsteps thud away. The kids start up yelling and screeching almost immediately and he hears the man laugh. A dark flare of anger spreads like magma through his lower stomach. If he had gone in, he'd have only tried to wreck their night so he walks away before he can think too hard about it.

The app says there's a meeting starting in ten minutes, so he gets in the car and drives the few streets over. In early sobriety, taquerías used to feel the way meeting rooms do now – little lighthouses in the dark – so there's a sad jab under the ribs when he drives over there, gets out, and finds the shutters down.

From behind him, half-way up the block, he hears an old man's voice shout, 'General Custer, the Fifth Battalion salutes you!' and he turns to see an old couple sitting on a couch in a grocery shop with barely any front and sides to it, just concrete columns covered in chipped red paint. They have blankets over their knees against the cold, their TV showing the sodden crowd of people waiting grimly for the grito in front of the Palacio Nacional, the palace and crowd lit up green and white and red. The few gaps of space on the Zócalo are slicked to an ice-rink shine by the rain tipping down. The old couple have a steaming clay cauldron of café de olla going, next to a plastic tray of conchas and croissants and cream-puffs.

'I told you it wasn't him,' one of the old women says, stopping her knitting to jab the man who shouted.

'Sorry,' the old man says, raising a hand. 'We thought you'd just been by. Was just a guy who looked like you.'

'Could have been twins,' says the old woman.

'Think he was looking for the meeting,' the old man says, with a backward nod. 'But they don't open on holidays.'

'Oh, it's OK,' he says, looking at the shuttered meeting-room, scratching his chin. He has a raw, deflated sort of ache in his chest. It's not that he wants to use. He just wants to talk, and not on the phone – he might like a hug afterwards, he doesn't know, and Adonai's been so grumpy lately.

The old woman who had been knitting is already starting to get up, lifting the blanket from her knees, dusting fluff from the velour of her tracksuit bottoms. 'Croissant, concha, what do you feel like?' she says.

'Whatever's going, honestly,' Diego says, and accepts a little clay cup and a concha in a napkin.

'You don't want cream on that lovely moustache,' she says, then sits back down to watch the president waving to the big crowds on the Zócalo.

Diego stands on the edge of the light, munching and dunking while the new president goes through the motions. They change the channel to the football highlights, the volume up so loud that they don't hear Diego lay his emptied cup down on the tiles or thank them.

Getting back into the car, Diego checks the time on his phone. If he pushes it, he can be at his mother's house in Aguascalientes before midnight, but he'll need something stronger than that café de olla to get him through, and pulls in at a convenience store. Diego gets out, stretches the tension out of his legs then looks over the railing. Here he sees a huge square lot like a prison-yard – teeming with drizzle under the hard white glare of security lights – full of lifesize plaster chefs. They are holding pizzas, gesturing to invisible customers, toting blank blackboards, their hats wobbly and full like flung white dough while they whisk or taste or chop vegetables. For a moment he loves them almost, the melted, earnest tenderness of their eyes, their unguarded smiles.

Diego is leaning on the railing now, balancing on his hands, when headlights flash twice and a car horn beeps.

He turns from the railing to see a huge jeep pulling in further up the road. The window is down, and Diego hears a voice say, 'Oh, thank God' in strangely-accented Spanish.

'I wasn't about to jump,' he says, dropping back onto his feet. 'Sorry, sorry.'

The guy at the window frowns and says, 'What? No. I thought I'd lost you.'

Diego takes a step back. He feels a crawl of dread.

'You were following me?' he says. He checks the distance between himself and the car. Could he sprint it?

'Not quite, no.' The guy in the jeep takes a cigarette out of a pack and lights up with a Zippo. 'I was looking for the meeting. But it was shuttered. When I went past the place again those old people told me my twin had also been by. They said you'd taken the Aguascalientes road. So I drove this way and, boom' – he lifts and drops his hand – 'here's my twin.' The driver's Spanish is good, but it's not his first language. He doesn't flatten the words out the way U.S. people do, but the slipped-gear noise of the 'j' could make him German or Dutch or something.

The driver squints at Diego and says, 'And, you know, facial hair aside, I'm not sure we even look that much alike.' The man tilts his head back against the car-seat and takes a no-handed suck of smoke, then billows it out with a big sigh of relief, saying, 'And frankly, chief, it would have been less weird if I hadn't pulled in. What's the twelfth step say?'

Diego scrapes his foot against the gravel and says, 'Yeah, alright', because this is the second-least strange and unpleasant thing to happen to him all day.

'We could smash a coffee in there,' the driver says, waving his cigarette at the convenience store. There's a hint of Central America in the accent, too, Diego hears now, and he can't help asking, 'Where'd you learn your Spanish?'

'I used to live here,' the driver says. 'Mexico City. Now I don't really know where I live. I just drive around. Doing jobs.'

'What kind?' Diego says, then wishes he hadn't, only then noticing the licence-plate says HONDURAS, which is when the driver laughs and says, 'What kind do you think?'

'Tourism,' Diego says quickly.

'Good answer,' the driver says, blowing out more smoke. 'How much clean time you got?'

'Like six years?'

The driver nods and says, 'Same.' He shrugs. 'Well. More or less.'

He turns off the ignition, puts up the window, then gets out of the car. 'Jesus,' he says, hugging his arms, even though he has a thick jacket on, one of those tan leather ones in old detective films. 'They're not lying, are they? Zacatecas is the coldest fucking state in the country.'

The driver gets his phone out and swipes the screen unlocked, the cigarette bobbing between his lips. 'I've got it all here – the Just for Today reading, the meeting protocols, all that. It's going to be quiet in there.' He juts his chin at the convenience store. 'What do you think? Do a meeting?'

'Good with me,' Diego says, his eyes moving towards the chefs in the lot at the bottom of the slope. Fuzzy halos of raindrops shine above them, rain pearling on their faces though he can't feel a drop. 'Be there in a second, OK? Just want to stretch the legs.'

'Yeah, man, no problem.' The driver sucks down the last of his cigarette in a single drag, before flicking the dying comet into the highway. 'What coffee you want?' he says, already walking across to the automatic doors.

'Whatever's fine, honestly. I'll follow you in. Just give me a minute.'

'Cool.'

The doors ping open and shut behind the driver. Diego goes back to leaning against the railing, the metal cool against the palms of his hands, lifts himself up off his feet. After a while, the rain cuts through the warm numbness and he crosses the forecourt and goes through the automatic doors. The driver's already sitting at a plastic table beside the hot drinks section, near a couple of truckers.

'It tastes kind of like tyre,' the driver says, holding out a black coffee.

'That's how you know it's efficient.'

'Yeah.' The driver pops open a bag of mini-donuts and tilts it towards Diego, then swipes his phone unlocked. 'You want to kick us off there?'

'Cool.' Diego clears his throat, takes the phone, and says, 'My name is Diego, and I'm an addict. This is a meeting of the Two Fucking Orphans in a Random 7/11 Group of Narcotics Anonymous.'

Scanners beep. The doors ping. Draughts chase around Diego's ankles. It's too cold to be walking around in espadrilles in Zacatecas. Forecourt smell blows in, and he thinks of his father's old workshop – that dark breath of oil, metal with maybe the ghost of soap and wool, too.

Diego gets to the end of his reading, says, 'Could someone please read "Who is an Addict?"' In the second before the driver begins to read from the screen of his phone, Diego thinks of his father moving about in the half-dark, a warm gone smile on his face as he tries to sing to the Beatles-hour on Radio Universal.

'You tripping out on me there, broseph?' the driver says.

'Oh, shit. Sorry. Yeah.' Diego opens his eyes.

He'll stop and look at that workshop before he goes to bed, he decides. His mother won't hear a thing.

'My name's Andrew, and I'm an addict,' says the driver, clearing his throat. Then he begins to read from the glowing screen of his phone, and Diego begins to listen.

He thinks of the stupid, heroic absorption of the chefs' smiles: was he so moved by that kitsch trash all of a sudden? He is – a little, maybe – his eyes smarting, his smile that of an idiot or an actor in a telecom ad. His moustache is beginning to look like those chef's moustaches. He huffs a laugh out through his nose, because these chefs seem to him for a moment poignant somehow, exemplary. They look like they're good at something.

SAINTS

When I get back from the bakery, I find Sandra – my former student from art school in Mexico City, my favourite student, in fact – standing on a chair and rummaging through the cupboards. This is not abnormal: it's the Easter holidays, so I've been half-expecting her to show up. She likes to decompress from her university teaching by blatting around the highlands on a thick-tyred bike with a pointed bonnet that looks like she's riding a red and white praying mantis.

The places she likes best aren't far from the small city I retired to. My son Carlos used to do more or less the same as she did. Sometimes I'd walk in the door and find him already there, reading on the garden chair. Sandra called late last night, saying she'd love to drop in on me if I was around. I was in the middle of scraping volcanic dirt from the robe of a wooden St. Joseph, and just said, 'Sure'. Company is good for me – like exercise, or vegetables. Though it doesn't stop it being strange to see her rooting through the cupboards.

'There must be something here somewhere,' Sandra is saying over her shoulder to two women sitting at my kitchen table with whom I'm only on nodding terms. They sometimes sell chiles and onions and tomatoes on blankets.

Sandra reaches on her tip-toes into the dark of the cupboard, and pulls out sad tubes of dried garlic powder and chili salt. She puts them down beside an egg I'd forgotten I had. She's also found one and a half slices of bread and a jar of Nescafé that's gone claggy.

'Hiya,' I say, laying the bakery bag down on the table.

The older one says, 'We're very sorry,' in Spanish, her voice soft, accented with an undersong of her indigenous language. She's wearing her hair in two grey plaits, over a black tabard embroidered with flowers. The dark nap of her skirt is zigzagged with pink and lilac threads, a sewn map to the fields of corn and dark mud that must lie around her town.

'You're here!' Sandra says, turning, 'Great! These women came to see you. I didn't have any money. So I just went to see if we had any food.'

I feel a twang at the word 'we', but this is the kind of thing Carlos used to do.

The older woman looks to the younger one, who nods and says, 'It wasn't really about food or money though.'

Across the kitchen, Sandra's hair is all mussed. She's still wearing pyjama pants and a Pixies t-shirt. She has the same twitchy attention she had in my tutorials, flicking through her notebook to quote my lectures back at me. She'd stand outside class, her face set hard before going in, as though it was a football match and she the captain of the team. The thought creeps over me that Sandra's wife, Teresa, must really look forward to her jaunts out of the country.

'We saw that you restore statues,' says the older woman.

'Yes. Saints, mostly,' I say.

'We have one for you,' the older woman says.

The younger woman rolls a large plastic bag down, exposing a craggy wooden sculpture of a bearded man in a broad-brimmed hat. It's just his head, neck, and torso, his arms smoothed away at the shoulders. As he comes into view, the older woman's face tenses. A look I know well.

'OK,' I say, and stoop to the statue, not looking at the older woman. There's a hole augured into the space where his mouth should be.

'Oh, wow,' Sandra says from across the kitchen. 'It's Maximón.'

Maximón doesn't deserve his bad reputation. He's a Mayan trickster god spliced with the saints of the colony, though this bust is one variant of many. There's the ones they do up like Al Pacino in *Scarface*, on a throne, granting favours, others who look like army generals, or draped in silk scarves. This Maximón is made of unvarnished wood. He's not in great shape.

'He was my son's,' the older woman says. 'He came off his scooter. He. Well. He used to look after this saint. Took a photo of his scooter to the chapel. Every year. Protection. And now. Well.' She cuts herself off, coughs, nods vigorously.

'We'd love to know how much you'd charge for a repair,' the younger woman says.

I run a finger over the buckshot of woodworm over its chest and face. A seam of rot-softened wood runs upwards through its shoulder. 'There's not much I can do to stop that ruining the thing eventually. But I can tease it out. Splice in a little bit of teak. Put stain on it. He'll look OK for a few more years.'

'And the charge?' the old woman says.

'There won't be one,' I say, holding my voice steady. I get to my feet. 'Three days OK with you?'

The older woman clasps my hands and thanks me. I can hear and feel the hard caps of worn skin on her fingertips against the calluses on my palms. Sandra slowly lifts the egg back into the cupboard.

'It's fine,' I say. There's an itch in my throat.

'Well,' the younger woman says, 'we'd better. You know.'

'Yes,' I say.

'Long journey,' the older woman says.

'Of course,' I say. I'm going to fall apart if they don't leave.

'Come back in three days,' I say.

'We're from near the lake,' the younger woman says, wagging a finger at the distance. 'Long way for us.'

'So you can keep him for us,' the older woman says, 'until the next time.'

'Or we can bring him,' Sandra says – the two women look at her like they'd forgotten she was there.

'All that way?' the older woman says, scratching the side of her chin.

'I can take him on my bike,' Sandra says.

'Hmm,' I say. I can picture the effect of the long motorcycle trip on my handiwork, can see the new wood shaking itself out on roads with the texture of crushed biscuits.

'Just a thought,' Sandra says.

'We'll figure that part out,' I say, even though I already have.

'We'd be so grateful,' the older woman says. 'You can bring him to the chapel, maybe.'

'Either way,' I say, 'We'll get him to you in three days or so.'

'Let me give you my number,' says the younger woman.

They back out of the kitchen, through the side-door that leads right into the street, shutting it behind them.

'That was so picturesque,' Sandra laughs from the other side of the kitchen.

'I suppose,' I say, watching them rejoin the bustle and dust of midmorning. They will jink past tuk-tuks, marching bands and gaggles of white tourists, to cram into a shuttle-bus, that will then rucket and bump over every hump in the road between here and Lago Atitlán. After that, what, a boat probably, out to one of the islands, then another tuk-tuk, more streetlife, more white tourists clogging the road, until finally they'll get back to a home where someone's been lost.

*

Maximón has irises but no pupils. The hole augered in for a mouth is all chapped around the edges. I pick at the wood with a finger. I am going to make every inch of him gleam.

Sandra helps me to lift the bust into my studio, then slips off to make a phone-call to her wife. I go to the garden for a moment. My house is a converted hacienda, the garden spreading through the centre. The air feels like warm water for a moment, like everything is happening at a hazed, muted distance, and I can't get the angles of anything to stay flush with anything else. *My son is dead and I miss him*, is the only thing I'm thinking even when I'm thinking about something else. I stand in front of the altar to Carlos I keep under the walkway that runs around the garden. It's a blown-up photo of him behind glass, framed in flowers that I change every season. Right now they're bird-of-paradise flowers, orange and purple and green spines that teem like thorns around the frame. The setup is level with the fountain and the iron table where he'd sit and read or draw when we'd come here on holidays. I had a bench laid with blankets for when he wanted to stretch out. Sometimes he'd nap. I'd hold him while he slept, feel his warmish snuffles on the palm of my hand and the tickle of his long hair. I wanted to touch his hair after he'd died, but the mortuary people wouldn't let me do anything more than say it was him. He had been tortured and shot at his apartment by a policeman who was working for a gang. The papers said it was his fault for sticking his nose in where he oughtn't – blame standing in for causation when nothing else is available. A bad meaning's less scary than none at all. I'd feared this happening when I lived in Guatemala in the 1980s, during the war, but the pain of it happening to my son was beyond any fear.

The mortuary attendant kept the sheet rolled down to just above his wounds. I saw a white diamond of scarring on his sternum and thought that I'd never know what had put that there. I wanted to dress him. In my mind I do dress him. I comb flat the long fibres of his bedsocks, the ones with individual toes in them, the ones that dunted my calf when he kicked in his sleep. I draw shut the string of his pyjama pants just under his little pot belly.

I look through the wedge of light falling from the big lamps over the bust of Maximón. He's standing on the bench.

'I am going to make you gleam,' I say aloud, then step into the tang of sawdust and metal shavings, and nudge shut the door with my ankle.

*

I am sitting in the living room, wiping dust from under my eye with a fingernail blackened with graphite. Sandra has my other hand pinned. She is saying, 'My wife sees ghosts all the time. I think it's fine. Normal, even.'

Sandra is looking at the little clay cup of café de olla I made. The spices are milder and the piloncillo blander than you get up north in Mexico, but it's enough to remind me of home. Crumbs of Spanish omelette are stuck to our plates – premade, bought from Costco, reheated.

'And what are your wife's ghosts like?' I ask, dabbing up wet crumbs of egg and potato with the end of one finger.

I follow Sandra's gaze to a Virgin Mary that stands in the corner, her hands clasped to her apple-red bleeding heart, in which are seven sabres plunged to their hilts.

'Just the people she dissects, I suppose,' Sandra says. She sounds a little spooked – anybody would in this house. 'Honestly, though, I think I just want to feel like it's normal. But it's just another thing that makes her impossible to talk to.'

'I'd love to see ghosts,' I say.

'If they're going to be anywhere, they're going to be here.' Sandra turns around to take in all the restored saints. Above her is the Saint Joseph that I finished off last night. I used so much lacquer and beeswax that my sinuses are still clogged.

'No offence,' Sandra says.

'None taken. Maybe I'm trying to summon a few ghosts. But it'd be hard given everything that happens around here. I'm not even the only woman you've met today who lost a son. Look at this guy,' I say, and toast the wooden bust of Maximón with my cup. His new layer of stain gives a dark molasses tang to the room.

'Yeah,' Sandra says, looking over at him. 'God. That was so heavy. I could feel the pain beaming out of them. I just threw everything I could find at them. I'm really sorry.'

'No, no.' I've felt clenched around that moment all day, resenting her for it, and now I feel something soften and open in my chest. 'It is heavy,' I say. 'Every time Carlos left the house, I'd get this tearing feeling. "Be careful out there," I wanted to say, every time, "that's a piece of my soul you've got there, walking around." That rip would only close when he came back through the door. And now he's never going to come through the door again – I don't know – it just stays open forever.'

'I get that with Teresa sometimes,' she says quietly. 'It makes me feel I'm an idiot.'

'We're all idiots. Love's a trap. That's how they get us to keep us coming back.'

'They?'

'Oh, you know,' I say, 'God. Contingency. Fate. Spirits. Saints.'

I look over at the twisted sandalwood window frames, feel their patterns begin to shift under my eyes, and then I breathe out, and the frames return again. I pat the limbless statue, feel the cool, hollow impact under my palm. 'You know how he ended up just a torso?'

Sandra shakes her head.

'It was a joke that got out of hand, a drinking game. He dared the sun to see how hot he could make himself. All the humans had their lymph and sweat and water and blood burned out of them, just a mass of beef jerky spread out on the burned desert of everything.'

Carlos used to point his camera at people in power and laugh at the danger he'd put himself in.

'And so Maximón rehydrated humanity by grinding up corn, fermenting the paste, making the first alcohol. Drinking it burns because it hurts to remember having been a paste. It's why people teeter when they're drunk.'

Sandra nods, her eyes narrowing.

'I really do appreciate your being here,' I say, then lay down my coffee cup and put my hand over my face. 'I need to make myself be around people.'

'I do too. You can really get sucked into just repeating the same day forever. You feel sort of haunted.'

Sandra is staring into the middle distance, her gaze passing through the shapes of smoke fraying up from her cup.

'You met someone else,' I say.

'Almost,' Sandra says. 'It wasn't as tempting as I thought. I went right up to the edge of doing something, and then I came back.'

'They're never worth it, affairs. I promise you.'

'I came to check in on you,' Sandra says 'and now we're talking about me. I always get so much out of these visits.'

'That's the way of it. And if you're a mother, you get filled up from filling people up. It's what we do.'

'You look like you're about to send me to bed.'

'I am, Sandra, I'm really sorry. The battery dies all of a sudden sometimes. I get these waves.'

Sandra stretches, yawning, and says, 'I'm flagging, too.' The wicker seat of her chair creaks as she presses herself up by the arms.

She pauses for a second, as if trying to decide to hug me, but then settles on a shy nod as she goes, just how she'd slip out of my tutorials.

I took Carlos to the aquarium in Monterey, California. He made otter noises, squeaking, skittering around the floor in front of the glass, trying to keep pace with their dark shapes scudding through the murk. I bought him a plush teddy otter holding a red starfish. 'Otitito!' he'd trill, throw him up, catch him. I kissed his forehead as he slept that night, imagining it falling in a golden snow, filtering somehow into his dreams. Then I stood and looked out at the bay. The town we were staying in had a huge cone-shaped stone lodged in the water: a volcanic plug. I saw shallow channels carved in it from millions of years of rain, mottled rust and olive where vegetation had caught.

Alone downstairs now in Antigua, I look through the curtains at a streetlamp whose glow teems with moths. Crickets are chirping nearby and dance music thuds out of the club up the road. From here I can see the blackened colonnades of an hacienda destroyed in an earthquake centuries ago.

I let the curtain fall. I turn back to look at Maximón. The edges of the hole bored in his face were all chipped when he came in, but I've smoothed them into a gleaming Cupid's bow.

*

The following morning, before Sandra is up, I give Pedro a call. He does jobs for me sometimes: light gardening, some transport, the occasional trip out to the sticks to price religious artefacts. I have a battered red Fiat station-wagon, and I can drive it: I just don't anymore. The grief can hit out of nowhere like the gust off a truck. It happens to me even if I'm walking. I'll have to duck into a church or a café and clutch my temples until I'm no longer dizzy. I can't let that happen on the road so my world is limited to those places I can get to on foot. I tell myself it's a phase but it's been two years, and I wonder if it could be the start of the end.

'Veronica,' Pedro says, when he picks up the phone. 'To what do I owe the pleasure?'

'Bit of work for you, if you want it,' I tell him, shaking coffee into the percolator.

Pedro clicks his tongue and says, 'God, I'd love to, Veronica. It's just my son.'

It's like someone's choked the breath out of me.

'What happened?' I say, and lower the packet of coffee to the counter.

'He broke his leg. Scooter.'

I have to sit down.

Last night, I dreamt I was in that sitting-room in Juárez. I was looking under the couch and found a hatbox. Inside, I found a golden bull, the metal shaped like shaggy hair and muscle. I lifted him, the neck clicking and sliding to one side, chin above shoulder. A noise like distant rain sifted from the bent neck, and, with it, the feeling something dreadful was about to happen.

'He's more embarrassed than hurt, really,' Pedro says. 'But I'm sort of waiting on him. I'm really sorry.'

'No, no, that's OK.' I try to press the tension out of my eyebrow.

'What's the job, anyway? So I'll know what I'm missing.'

'Up to Atitlán,' I say, my eyes shut. I can feel Maximón's eyes boring through the walls at me. I need him out of here already. 'One of the islands.'

He clicks his tongue. 'Oh, that's such a beautiful part of the country. I'm jealous.'

'Yes, well, we'll have to find a way, won't we.'

'Sure. Hey, look, I think I'd better go. You OK for everything?'

I open my eyes, look out the window, see a tiny green lizard go skiting up one of the columns that surround the garden.

'Bit of gardening, maybe. But only when it's calmer over there.'

'Will do.'

The lizard vanishes into a crack, tail whipping.

'Get well soon,' I say, and I haven't even pressed *End* before I hear Sandra's flip flops in the hall. She yawns in the doorway. There is a mild odour of weed.

'I can drive, you know,' Sandra says, opening the bag of yesterday's croissants – now almost completely black with leaked grease – and placing two in the microwave. 'It doesn't bother me.'

'I hate needing this much help.'

'It's normal.'

The microwave beeps.

'So,' says Sandra, sliding out the plate. She finds paper napkins and a pair of knives, then brings them over. 'Where are we off to?'

'Right here,' I say, sliding over to her the receipt that the younger woman left yesterday. An address is written in red pencil over the faded prices of chayote, tomato, onion, chile verde.

Sandra puts the address into her phone. A red tangle appears, joining Antigua to a little dot on the lake. 'Nice,' Sandra says, pinching the zoom inwards. 'Only three hours.'

'Those poor women,' I say. 'Coming all this way.'

'Well, then we can do them a favour,' Sandra says, over the whistling of the kettle. This time I'm up and over before she can get to it.

'If we leave now,' Sandra says, tapping at her phone, 'we'll be back well before sunset. So it's up to you.'

I fill the cafetière, listen to the bubbles as they rise to the brim. I take it to the table, wipe my hands, and I say, 'Yes. OK. Let's do it.'

*

Getting out of the town always feels like the longest part of the drive. The car jolts as Sandra stops for a couple of dozy white tourists. Maximón shunts forwards and then backwards in the seat behind us, the plastic bag over him rustling against his seatbelt.

'Kim Jong-Un has the right idea,' I say.

'Which one?' says Sandra.

'Banning tourists,' I say.

'Jesus. Harsh.'

We slow along the tourist-drag gauntlet of shisha bars, cafés with tasselled curtains for doors, clubs where they put old saints in glass boxes above the dancefloor, their eyes and hands upcast to heaven.

My eyes feel sandy from lost sleep. 'I just get nervous, taking this road. When I first got here, it was checkpoint, checkpoint, checkpoint.'

'During the war?'

I nod. 'Peace Corps. Bad time to do that. Everyone thought we were spies.'

'I mean,' Sandra says, wavering her hand back and forth in the air.

'Well, yeah, I'm sure everything we said filtered up someplace able to use it. I have atoned for it,' I add, unsure how many levels of irony it contains.

'Can you do that?'

'You can try.'

I point out the windscreen, sweeping my finger back and forth, to the right, the land falls away to empty country, lush fields, thick woods, all the way to the blue outlines of old, dead volcanoes.

'The war felt like it was everywhere,' I tell Sandra.

'Mexico City's getting like that,' Sandra says. 'I remember my first date with Teresa. Well. First *date*-date. Going to an exhibition my brother had, standing at the pedestrian crossing, holding hands, and this police pickup goes barrelling past, cops in the back over these guys with zipper-tied wrists.'

'It's like the war. Nothing you could understand except a trepidation. My host family were antique collectors. I'd help out a bit. I remember how skinny the guerrillas were under the weight of their Makarovs, how afraid they were of me. The army, the police, with their American sunglasses. On these forest roads you could just vanish. All kinds of things done to the bodies, you know. Twisting ropes until heads burst, gutting people, winding their innards around tree-trunks.

'Now they get the ultraviolence from videogames,' Sandra says, breaking off the end of the croissant she's brought out with her. 'But back then, what? CIA manuals?'

'No,' I say, '*The Lives of the Saints*.'

*

The worst of the day's heat has passed. Sandra drives down the slope towards the little dock and the ferries that go out to the islands that stud Lago Atitlán. Through the trunks of the fir trees late yellow light glimmers on the blue water. The last hundred-odd yards are slow because we're stuck behind a religious procession. A big flayed Jesus bobs at the head of the crowd. Men push wheeled frames of Roman soldiers, the Devil bobbing from a high rope, paint showing his ribs, avid eyes, a giggling mouth. Trumpets and drums. Pools of smoking red wax drip behind the train of men and women and children making their way along the lakeshore, white tourists filming on their phones.

'I always feel,' Sandra says, 'people in those ceremonies are all a bit "We got him" about Jesus.'

I follow the crucifix with my eyes.

'Like, imagine being local, sitting in the dark behind the rows of rich people in the old churches, gold shining under candlelight – you're hearing everyone talking in a language you don't understand, and then when you go outside, seeing your people marched away to prisons or scaffolds – well, I don't know – like they're all being killed the way he was. For them he's a warning.'

We get onto the boat, joining the after-school rush, mothers and grannies chivvying kids into orange life-jackets, teenagers slapping each other and squawking.

'Homeward bound,' Sandra says to Maximón. I am pillowing his head on a life-jacket when the boat's motor putters into life, chugging us through the thick scab-coloured algae. At the second island we get out, get into the first tuk-tuk we find and zoom up a steep dry maze of streets that smell of diesel-oil and freshly cut cilantro. In front of us, a kid on a bike carries a fish impaled through the gills on the tines of a palm-frond. Water drips from the fish's tail, the scales still with their gold tint, the gills a scarlet that feels sharp to look at.

'Servidas,' the tuk-tuk driver says, slowing up outside a faded orange house. A metal sign curves above the door, the words COFRADÍA DEL CRISTO SEPULTADO. A rainbow of fairy lights blinks on and off above the dark cave of the doorway.

'Wow,' says Sandra, as we get down. She's carrying Maximón sideways in her arms.

'You don't have to come in,' I say, and pay the driver.

'I—' Sandra begins, eyeing the reddish smoke that clouds the doorway. A woman who must be in her eighties is sitting in the doorway, shaking a red dish of plastic up at us. Sandra foosters a coin out of her little zippy purse. 'Yeah. Are you sure?'

'I won't be long,' I say. The driver's a heavyset man in his fifties with a white beard. He gives me a thumbs up and says, 'Sure, I'll take you back.'

Sandra hands me the bagged saint. He feels light in my arms as I turn and walk into the incense. The darkness smokes around me, lilac-tinted in the fleeting electric lights. Through the deep, foresty sugar-cloy of copal there's the clean sting of Lysol from the bare concrete floor still dark with recent washing. I feel a tingling in the skin of my throat, but it's not fear, it's more like that second-day-of-school feeling, when you're unsure if yesterday's faces are going to be there.

I get to the end of the corridor. Here are two rows of benches set into a craggy space carved out of the wall. Most people here are women my age, telling rosary beads, talking in low voices, looking towards the altar behind a brass rail. There's an empty cane chair at the centre, the back draped in a red cloth.

Some turn, smiling – it's strange some old white woman has shown up. Their voices are gentle, praying in this local language, its quizzical uptick at the end of a phrase. I just stand there, cradling Maximón, feeling the weight of him assert itself. The altar's clustered with little glass bottles of tamarind-flavour Quetzalteca liquor, stacked-up packets of Marlboro Red. Smaller plaster saints – Bernadette, Anthony, Martin, Jude – stand clustered at the foot of the chair. The back walls are busy with framed photos of families, of houses, of businesses, scraps of paper set into their corners. I peer among them, see a photo of a turquoise imitation Vespa, a smiling young man with a parting shaved into his hair holding the handlebars, and Maximón grows heavy in my arms. Walking towards the altar, more heads turn, until, as I near the brass rail, I see her at last: dressed all in black, wearing pearls, her hair loose and straggling to her shoulders.

'You came,' she says, clasping my hands that are holding the bag.

I kneel to lay down the statue. 'Let me know what you think.'

She kneels with me, rolling the bag down from the saint's head and shoulders. Some sigh and others click their tongues. I watch her run her finger along the teak scar I've laid in the saint's cheek.

'There was no way to hide the scar,' I say, 'so I just made it pretty instead.'

'It is pretty.'

Now she runs her hands over the places I've smoothed away the woodworm. Her eyes watch the movement of her fingers, going over lips gleaming with the stain I laid on. In the candle-flames he seems to breathe.

'He's perfect,' she says, her hand now resting on the solid curve of one shoulder. 'I can't thank you enough.'

'It was a pleasure,' I say, and my voice is tight.

'You can put him back, if you want,' she says, standing up. 'Bring him to his chair.'

'Oh, I couldn't possibly,' I say. 'I'm just a visitor.'

'No, you're a friend.' She balls up the plastic sacking in her hands. 'This is your house anytime now. Just ask for me. My name's Elizabeth.'

'Veronica's my name.'

'It's a pleasure. Don't let this be the last time. Now, please.' She gestures towards the altar. 'Do us the honour.'

'OK,' I say, and I'm nervous again, lifting Maximón this last time. He is calmer now, a blank light, like water, or air, or God, maybe. I move through the dimness toward the shifting curtain of smoke. I smell Carlos hugging me, sweaty from his journey, from coming to see me as fast as he could. A woman lifts the rail. I look back at the mother, her hands clasped. I go past the cigarettes and the bottles and the cluster of small chipped saints. I lower Maximón to his chair, hear the creak of the wicker seat, its back draped with silk scarves: turquoise, lilac, a deep, rose gold. I can feel the eyes of the room on me. I pick up the first scarf, rub the cool nap between my finger and my thumb. The saint looks up at me. His moustache looks combed, his beard and hair, too. My chest is cool and dry. There's a flash of the ruined cathedral on my street, its broken ceilings letting in the blue light. I put one hand on the saint's wooden shoulder. Though it is not my son, he still needs love. So I pat his shoulder, give him a smile, and begin to dress him.

BODIES

Done cutting for the day, Teresa takes the lift up from the mortuary, goes out of the police precinct and to her car, scraping crud from the corners of her eyes. There have been forest-fires again this year. Springs nowadays burn far worse than summers ever did, air rank with the bang of cindered grass.

Her phone buzzes. It's Sandra.

'You OK?' Teresa says.

'I fucked up.' Sandra's voice is a groan.

'How?'

'Dinner. I didn't put it on. I fucked up. I got all lost in what I was reading.'

Ahead and around, the overpasses and highway tunnels interlock and flow in grey lattices, like coloured diagrams of chest-muscle. Cyclists zip past her in face-masks. Under the hazy blue light, the faded shop-fronts and cantinas like old photos of themselves. Teresa curses at the thought of a long drive home to an empty fridge.

'Are you mad at me?' Sandra says.

'What? No. There was someone pulling out. Car. Asshole.'

'I should let you go.'

'Don't worry about it,' says Teresa, pacing from one bumper of her car to the other. She blows out a breath, a hand on her hip, then adds, 'You know what, I reckon I should go see my brother.'

'Really?'

'I mean why not. He won't have food either.'

'Ouch.'

'At least this way I can remind him to eat. What are you going to have?'

'I don't know. Probably go to that felafel place across the road. Get you something?

'That stuff never fills me up. No.'

'Alright. Jesus.'

'I'll see you in a while,' Teresa says. 'Love you. Going to drive now.'

'Yeah. OK.' Now Sandra's voice is all bunched and shut. 'You too.'

A cloud shifts and the light goes a brown like iodine. She'd sometimes go with her father on trips to get car-parts, sit with him in his hotel room trying to spot birds: papamoscas with their lime-green punk tufts, the degollados with red bibs like a spill of blood, the gorriones, sootier and skinnier than those back in Aguascalientes.

Teresa takes a deep breath, shuts her eyes for a moment, and gets into the car. The kid whose autopsy she spent the day on is beside her in the passenger seat, the stitches of his 'Y'-incision treacle-dark in the streetlight. His skin is electric-white, the brightness of his body brightening and darkening with a rhythm almost like a heartbeat.

She gets in beside him. He'd tried to rob an Oxxo and got himself shot. The ghosts are not unusual. Once she had a torso moaning beside her all the way home. Another time, a young girl they'd pulled out of Río de los Remedios, her head wobbly and greenish like an old football had come with her to work, telling Teresa everything that she expected to find out in her autopsy. Most of the time their presence makes her feel serene; she likes talking to them, although she never does it aloud.

Today's kid gives her a brisk salute.

'You did a beautiful thing here,' he says, lifting his dirt-straggled hair to show the needlework holding his scalp on. 'Can barely see the crater.'

'It's literally my job,' Teresa says, and reverses out of the precinct car-park.

The kid was lying in a pool of head-blood and Coca-Cola. Held loosely in his hand was a kitchen knife – purple handle, serrated blade, the same kind she and Sandra have at home, that they dice onions with.

'Still means a lot,' the kid says, easing his seat back with a crunch.

Not all of the dead she works on follow her out of the mortuary.

'What was it?' the kid says.

'About what?' Teresa says.

'About my face.'

'Just a shit day,' she says.

'Tell me about it,' says the kid. She's given him a deeper voice than he probably had – his vocal cords weren't that long or thick. She needs someone who talks to her like that.

'I don't know,' she says, waiting at the stop-lights, one foot on the dash. 'You remember that other guy working on you, don't you?'

The kid nods.

'Rubén,' he says.

'He gets to me. His smell. Delicados. That used to be my brand. I could smoke a whole fucking pack right now.'

'Right.'

'And he was all jittery, you know? I love cutting, being around you. But someone like him bouncing around the room or whatever, it knocks me right off-stride, you know?'

'He's brusque, too.'

'Rude, yeah. I don't know. I feel like he's been reading those 'How to Pick Up Girls' books. You know – "be rude", "wear better glasses". Because he got the glasses and started being rude around the same time.'

'You were hungry, too.'

'Still am,' Teresa says as the lights change and they begin to cruise again. The hunger feels like a suction in her throat. 'And I'm fairly sure Sandra won't have any food ready for us at home.'

'Not very responsive,' says the kid. He is looking out the window, the streetlights in the blue dark look like people stooping to peer in.

'She's doing a PhD.' Teresa says. ' I don't want to be one of those fuckers who's like "Oh, it's not real work, you're sitting home all day".'

'But.'

'But I woke up from a horrible dream this morning, and I just wanted some fucking Coco Pops. Put the TV on, zone out, like it's a Saturday and I'm six again. Except there weren't any left, because Sandra. So when the call came in to get you, I just left – without eating or saying goodbye or whatever, telling her something, you know?'

'And wound up hurting yourself.'

'She didn't even notice. She's used to me not being there. You know, all day, that gritting noise of the scalpel moving through you, made me think of the noise when you bunch cilantro together and cut it. Everything I took out of you and put on those blue boards, it made me think of food.'

'That's crazy.'

'And Rubén standing beside me, with his cigarette-smell.'

'You used to smoke.'

'No. Yes. Different brand. Rubén's cigarettes were my father's. I used to wear his old jacket over my clothes in university.'

'You've a twitch as well.' The kid taps under his left eye. 'Here.'

'You think I can't feel it?'

'Like it's about to jump off. Like a frog's leg.'

She clicks her tongue. 'Fuck, man, I just want to get home and find the windows running with condensation from all the pots, you know? Sandra shredding meat, bones and skin steaming and bubbling in the caldo de jitomate.'

'You're even making me hungry,' the kid says, 'and I don't even have any of the... ah, hardware.'

'Sorry about that.' Teresa says, hands gripping the wheel. They speed down a tunnel decorated all over the sides and ceiling with paintings of mackerel, and the whoosh of their speed and the zip of the images really does feel like an undersea moment.

'Her hair flops all over the place. So I got her this black bandana for when she's cooking.'

'Which is rarely.'

'But it *does* happen, you know. Makes her look like she's in ISIS, that bandana. She does this bit where she puts a finger in the air, gives the wall a spaced-out-looking stare, like the guys in videos.'

'She's funny.'

'Yeah, I love her. She just pisses me off sometimes.'

The kid is looking at her, with a floaty steadiness in his eyes. He's kind of hovering in his seat.

'What?'

'Just wanted to say thanks.'

'For what?'

'Hugging me.'

'Oh. That. Yeah.'

'You undid the straps holding my body, got my arms out. You smoothed my fingers, wiggled the thumb, undid all the stiffness. You patted my hip. And then, when Rubén turned away you hugged me.'

Teresa doesn't say anything. The streetlights go foggy for a moment.

'You looked like my brother. He slept rough, too, you know.'

'Back before he got it together.'

'I thought he never would. He smelled like you: bins, old socks, paint-thinner.'

'Sorry.'

'Not your fault. You never had a chance.'

'I saw my brother trying to sleep in Jardín Pushkin, too skinny to get comfortable on the wood. The day the truck dropped on our father, my mother called me and told me. I went out to the garden to find him but he was chasing across the back field after our dog. I couldn't catch him so I just kept shouting, "Dad's dead, Dad's dead, come back!" When he realised it wasn't a joke the colour just washed out of his face and he dropped to the grass like a stone.'

'That was why you held me.'

'My chest hurts same now like I was running after him again.'

'Acid reflux.'

'Sure.'

She worked the blade beneath the kid's jawline, loosening the skin enough to slide the tongue and windpipe down into the chest cavity. Then she pried apart an upper section of the aorta so Rubén could shine in a torch, grunting as he sheared open the sternum for her to lift out the thoracic cage, the liver, the viscera. She nudged her way through the loose parcel of organs, dark things going pale, pale things going greyish, greenish, the blood leaching downwards.

Clapping the emptied-out frame of a car, her father would say, 'I never know what part I take out that makes a car not a car anymore, you know?' She'd hand him wrenches, hold things in place while he wound bolts flush with the metal. She loved the smell of the place: metal shavings, petrol, sweated-in old denim.

'I felt for you when I got to the pills.'

'Benzos.'

'Yeah. I mean. That's really how you died.'

'I wasn't even holding the knife that hard. I was tottering, more begging than threatening. It was for the street, it wasn't for the shop, I just didn't have any belt-loops left on my trousers to put it in, you understand. I didn't know they were restocking the ATM. Otherwise I wouldn't have gotten my head blown off.'

'It wasn't blown off. Top of the head, towards the back. If they come and find you I think it'll be an open casket.'

'Felt pretty blown off to me. A weird last second – sudden angles of light, a bang I heard but couldn't feel. I thought it was just the noise of falling to the floor. But, well.'

'Here we are.'

'Here you are, anyway. I don't know where I am.'

'You're dead,' she says quietly.

The kid just brightens and darkens, brightens and darkens. When Teresa turns her head, it's just the streetlights swiping in white lines above her, little coughs of breeze puttering through the half-open window, before she rises out of the tunnel and into her brother's neighbourhood.

She takes the elevator up. At the end of the corridor she sees Diego waiting at the door of his apartment, ferns in gravel beds all along the corridor.

'Nice,' she says.

'And how about this fly-as-hell faux-marble, eh,' says Diego. He's wearing striped grey chef's trousers and a black shirt. He hugs her at the door.

'This neighbourhood is so crazy for you,' she says. 'There's nothing here.'

'That's not fair. There's supermarkets. And pensioners.'

'Oh, wow.'

'I'm on a boredom kick. Closer every day to becoming a monk.' He bumps the door wider with his hip, then holds it for her as she ducks through.

'Have you any food?' Teresa says. The apartment is dimly lit with cracked floorboards, warped skirting-boards, and old, comfy-looking furniture.

'I don't think you'll like the menu,' he says. 'No animals were harmed in the making of it.'

There's an acetone rawness to the air in the room.

'Smells like my job in here,' she says.

'Look like it, too?' He gestures to the large empty room, through which white streetlight is spilling down over a cluster of bodies, splayed in the geometries of sleep on white sheets.

'They're still wet,' he says. 'I still have to stick on the nails and hair and stuff.' He walks over to the body nearest the door, shaped like a man, lying in the pose of a body from Pompeii.

It's a copy of Diego, down even to the hairs on his chest and the little scar by his navel. There's a poppy collar of bruises around his forearm and a needle shoved into the high, blue veins of the inner fold of his elbow, like any of the OD victims she's seen.

Diego unsockets the arm and waggles it at her. She slaps it away.

'Are they realistic, though?' he says. 'Their poses, I mean.'

Diego's plastic face peers up at her in its rictus.

'Do I have to look at all of them?' she says, taking in the room full of bodies under sheets, their clean, mellow glow in the lights.

'Sorry,' says Diego. 'It's a bit much.'

'What made you do it?'

Diego sucks his teeth and flips his hair back from his forehead. She imagines dark stitches all along the hairline.

'There's a pretentious version in the catalogue,' he says. 'But I think it's like those ex-voto things: paintings after a near-death experience with a prayer thanking Jesus or God or Mary or whoever for saving them. They show the thing that *didn't* happen, cars on fire, or drowning bodies, getting stabbed, whatever. Over them you've got this saint coming down from the clouds, intervening, stopping it. All that. Kitsch and gruesome all at the same time. I look for them whenever I'm poking around a church or whatever. There's one of a guy dying of an OD, marinating in a pool of Xanax and red wine with the Virgin Mary above it. And I saw myself there, like I was a dish being cooked up for God or something.'

'And that was it,' Teresa says.

Diego gestures at the bodies. 'All the times I nearly died. Not just drugs, either: there's one on my first fucking sober holiday in Sayulita when I nearly got sucked out to sea by a riptide.'

Teresa watches his gaze move over the sheet-covered body in the far corner. He's tugging at the skin of his chin, his gaze lost and preoccupied.

'I guess it's a way of saying sorry,' he says.

He's still holding the arm, its fingers brushing the floorboards.

Teresa kneels to look into the gap in the nearest body to her. Its inside is a shiny beige hollow. She puts a hand into the gap, feels a humid shadow drop over her skin.

'Those are like the opposite of my bodies. Empty.'

He's leaning against the door, his arms folded. The look on his face is proud.

She gives a chin-jut at the other bodies. 'And the rest?'

'This one's me after I nearly got washed into a storm-drain. And that's if I'd gotten shot the time I was robbed, you remember?'

She nods, numbly.

'I didn't mean to bring it all back for you, he said. 'I just want to get it out of me, all that stuff.'

They look from sheet to sheet. There are three more he hasn't even described.

'Here, I'm parched after that drive, you have a Coke or something?'

'Ah, I'm a shit host. Sorry.'

He's filling a glass at one of those Japanese water filters.

'When did you get it together enough to buy one of these?'

'I am growing and changing,' he says, intoning like he's on an infomercial.

He goes to the fridge and stoops into it.

'And food in the house and everything.'

He puts a plastic tub of hummus on the black tiles of the sideboard, then takes out pan arabe and another tub of felafel.

'This OK with you?'

'Sure.'

'Cool, because I have fucking nothing else.'

He slides the bread and felafel into the oven, then stands there tapping his foot as the timer ticks. Under the light she can see the white pinpricks on his arms against the black of the tattoos he's gotten since getting sober – cormorants, a heron, a crown of thorns. Like some kind of swap. They think that way, recovery people, in big, obvious symbols.

'Did you have a ghost with you today?'

She nods.

'It follow you home?'

'He. And yeah.' She gets to her feet, dusting her knees off. 'Ghosts are good listeners.'

'Can't imagine how.' He puts on a theatrical voice. "You mean you've had a bad day? *I'm* the one who's dead." What was today's body, then?'

'Bit like you.'

'Junkie, then,' he says.

'Diego.'

'What? I'm allowed to say the word. How's life beyond the morgue?'

She shrugs.

'Weird dreams. I think it's the heat. Had one about Dad.'

Diego gives her a steady look.

'What was he doing?' Diego says, and swirls his glass, the ice-cubes clacking.

'Just looking. At the fields. You know the way he did. Actually, wait.' She taps the front of her forehead. 'Today, I was rinsing off the blood and the drains were gurgling.

It was Dad watering a black oak at the foot of the garden, this cloud of starlings over his head.'

'That's beautiful,' Diego says. 'How'd he seem?'

'I don't know. Sad, I suppose.'

Diego looks at the tiles, raps them with his knuckles. He makes a crease of his mouth, then nods. Behind him, the glass of the oven door is filming over with smoke.

'You sure those aren't burning?' Teresa says.

'Nah, it's fine. Honestly, have a l – Oh.'

He opens the door. The smoke billows up, smelling of scorched herbs. The blackened felafel steams. The flatbreads are dark frisbees of ash.

'Shit,' he says.

'How high do you have that thing turned up?'

'Oh, all the way. I was impatient.'

'You know that's not how it works?'

'It isn't? Fuck. I'm really sorry.' He pokes with a fork at the felafel. 'Hey, but some of these look OK. Eat around the burned bits?' He pops a whole felafel in his mouth, says, 'Oh, shit,' wafting air into his mouth. He chews for a second, stops, then goes to the bin to spit.

'Oh, God,' he says. 'Like bits of volcano.'

Teresa sighs. 'It's OK,' she says.

'Fuck, man, I never have guests.' He points, says, 'You want another glass of that?'

'You're spoiling me.' She holds out the glass.

'You doing anything this weekend?' he says, as he refills.

She shakes her head, accepting the glass.

'Why?' she says.

He turns away, leaning his cheek against his shoulder, watching what looks like a thistle-seed turning through the light, although it's probably just a dust-mote.

'I'm not sure I can spoil the surprise,' he says. 'But you'll like it. I swear.'

'No bodies?'

'Not even fake ones,' he says.

Teresa shrugs, says, 'Sure, yeah. Why not.'

*

On Saturday, Teresa wakes up nervous. There's a text on her phone from Diego: he's already on his way over. Outside, Sandra is up watering the garden, the hose between her legs like she's pissing. When she hears the door click open, she shouts 'Dracarys!' and turns up the blast of the water.

'I'm off,' Teresa says.

'La otra?' Sandra doesn't look up from the watering.

'Ha, ha. I won't be long.' Teresa pushes up the long bit of hair over Sandra's nape and kisses her between the forking tendons. Things are OK again. After Diego's the other night, Teresa got home to the 'apology tacos' Sandra got from the overpriced place in La Roma. They had sex afterwards, that dreamy, half-asleep kind where nobody comes but nobody minds.

On the drive to the campus, Teresa watches the smoky motion of clouds reflected in bonnets, windscreens, the windows of a new shopping centre. She parks over at the biggest sculpture in the Espacio Escultórico, a big ring of concrete obelisks set diagonally into the ground patch of parched grass and volcanic rock that has weeds poking out of it. Diego is waiting there, near some students who are lounging in the centre of the circle, wearing pilled Radiohead and Grinderman t-shirts and passing a joint around.

'So, is this the plan?' Teresa says. 'Stand here, get a contact high from those kids?'

Diego shakes a head, wagging a finger at the big stone circle.

'OK, so, you and your ghosts, yeah?'

'Yeah.'

He nods.

'OK. So I had one, too. Not long ago. And, like, I don't know if Dad was actually there or if it was just my brain – you know what I've done to that thing. But I came here the other week, and I don't know what it was, but it felt he was really there, you know? That old leather jacket. All that stale smoke. Delicados. Faros. But right then I wanted them. And then he was there, sort of.'

He didn't even look at their father at the funeral, and here he is, with visitations. But then she sees the worry in his eyes, feels again the shock of looking in the dead kid's eyes and seeing Diego's.

'This fucking air, man. Even here, right?' Diego says, rubbing his throat. 'I feel like I've got a papercut in here.'

Teresa counts around the circle of obelisks.

'Which one did you climb?' she says.

'Fourth one in,' Diego says, already beginning to walk towards it.

The rock is warm under Teresa's back as she lowers herself down beside Diego, her view rising from puffs of smog to gleaming towers and on to a sheer blue square of nothing framed by the sculpture. She tilts her head back and points to a grey cloud that looks like a manta-ray.

'Don't worry. That's part of it. I checked the forecast.' Diego slides a box of Delicados from his inside jacket pocket. 'Happy Christmas.'

'Are you serious?' Teresa looks at the box without tearing off the cellophane wrapper.

'Yeah. Didn't bring a lighter, though. Assuming you have one.'

'You fucker,' Teresa says, but she's laughing.

Diego taps his nose.

'Giving up smoking.'

'It's for quitters,' Teresa says, then tears off the wrapper, undoes the foil, and hands Diego the lighter.

He lights up and puffs a couple of clouds into the air.

'What's the point not smoking, when the air's so fucked anyway.' He hands the lighter back.

'Yeah.' Teresa turns the lighter wheel slowly, so it sparks, then lifts her head towards the flame, and watches the strands of smoke from her cigarette knit in with the smoke from Diego's.

A long drop of rain bursts on her forehead, then another, and another. The kids sitting on the ring around the dry grass scarper, and then it starts to bucket down properly.

'OK,' Diego says, sitting up, pulling up her hoodie. 'Showtime.' He slides on his ass down the obelisk.

Teresa follows him into the lee of the stone they've been lying on, where they hunker and look out at the rain's phosphor seethe. The din is too loud for them to talk, which suits her fine, the sheeting rattle of drops on metal and concrete like a muffled roar from years ago. She was six when she and her mother went to join him on one of his trips to Mexico City. They'd travelled south through roaring white air, past warehouses, lit signs, black stretches of empty road, her chest all tight euphoria at the thought of him waiting for them there: but then something happened, and he hadn't been able to meet them at the station as planned. Even in the cinema later, when he still hadn't shown, she'd had that loose, raggedy fear; but then, sitting in the dark, there'd been a suck and a puff of cold air – the screening-room door opening, a rectangle of light all down the aisle, and there was her father, head poked in, squinting, row by row, until at last his gaze fell on her, his face softened, and down he marched down towards her, in his cold smell of rained-on leather and Palmolive soap, right at the bit where Scar's hyenas were marching back and forth, and he laughed at how hard she hugged him and said, 'It's only a film, Tere, don't worry, it's only a film,' his voice barely audible over the rain drumming on the cinema roof.

'Well?' Diego has one eye shut against the smoke rising up across his face. He's smiling a little. That plus the tache plus the shut eye, it makes him look like a smug pirate. 'Working for you?'

'It will if you shush.'

'Sorry, Tere.'

'It's OK.' She shoulders him, but gently. 'Now – shush.'

A white mist of rain breaks cold over her cheeks and bare wrists, like cigarette smoke climbing a projector's cone of light, and, for a second, it's like a door's about to open in that fog, and her father's about to appear, his head moving as he half-jogs down the slope to their seats, then he steps sideways along their row towards them, softly, through the dark.

Acknowledgements

First and foremost thanks to Ben Pester, who helped me see that I should give this writing short fiction thing a shot, for reading an entire early draft, and for painstakingly, one story at a time, showing me how it's done.

Huge thanks to Tom Conaghan for taking this collection on and teaching me more than I could imagine: still so amazed and surprised.

Unending gratitude to Quinnie Tan for her love and support, for keeping me sane, for making me laugh; to Hugo and Eva for the constant amusement; to my mother, father, and sister for their encouragement, love, support.

Early versions of these stories appeared in the *Dublin Review*, *Lonely Crowd*, *South Circular*, *The Fence*, and *The Tangerine*: my thanks to Brendan Barrington, John Lavin, Jane Fraser, Kieran Morris, John Phipps, Charlie Baker, and Aoife Walsh for their work on them.

My thanks go to May-Lan Tan, Wendy Erskine, Cathy Sweeney, Paul Whyte, and Colin Barrett for helping me wrestle with the short-story form.

The Arts Council of Ireland issued generous support to me in the completion of this collection: my thanks go to them also.

Doctor Bob, Bill W., Jimmy K., and friends – definitely not saints, but the best storytellers out there for sure.